PATH
of the
SHE-WOLF

THERESA TOMLINSON

RED FOX

A Red Fox Book

Published by Random House Children's Books
20 Vauxhall Bridge Road, London, SW1V 2SA

A division of The Random House Group Ltd
London Melbourne Sydney Auckland
Johannesburg and agencies throughout the world

Copyright © text Theresa Tomlinson 2000

1 3 5 7 9 10 8 6 4 2
First Published by Red Fox 2000

This book is sold subject to the condition that
it shall not, by way of trade or otherwise, be lent,
resold, hired out, or otherwise circulated without the
publisher's prior consent in any form of binding or cover
other than that in which it is published and without a
similar condition including this condition being imposed
on the subsequent purchaser.

The right of Theresa Tomlinson to be identified as the author
of this work has been asserted by her in accordance with
the Copyright, Designs and Patents Act, 1988.

Printed and bound in Denmark by
Nørhaven A/S

Papers used by Random House
are natural, recyclable products made from wood grown in
sustainable forests. The manufacturing processes conform to
the environmental regulations of the country of origin.

The Random House Group Limited Reg. No. 954009
www.randomhouse.co.uk

ISBN 0 09 940 2653

Contents

Prologue

It was early in December: a bright chill morning. Marian strode through Barnsdale Woods carrying bundles of herbs on her back. She was exhausted and saddened for she'd spent the night nursing a sick man, only to see him die as dawn came. She slowed her steps and looked about her seeking consolation from the woodlands that she loved.

Great swathes of grass were blanched with frost. A few small patches stood out bright green where sun came spiking starlike through the trees. Those glorious patches steamed with mist. Marian's spirits lifted and she stretched out her fingers to touch the stiff white fur of frost that coated branches and twigs. The brown bones of last summer's bracken glistened in the sharp sun.

A distant regular thud told her that the coal diggers had started their work, and a tiny weasel shot across her feet into the cover of dried ferns. Suddenly Marian stopped. Instinctively, she stood as still and rooted as the trees that surrounded her while a dark shape emerged

1

from the undergrowth. It was a she-wolf. The creature leapt silently across her path; passing in an instant.

Marian was not afraid, for the wolf had no interest in a tired, middle-aged wisewoman. But long after it had gone she still stood there, seeing again the sleek brown-grey coat, the floating tail, the ripple of powerful muscles beneath the fur. The she-wolf travelled through the wintry woods at speed, calmly going about her business.

Marian set off again, her step a little lighter, knowing that she too must go her own way, follow her own path.

1

Brig's Night

It was the first night of February. Magda crept away from the Forestwife's cottage into the woods, after dusk. She was a strong young woman of twenty years, very tall in stature with a great mane of chestnut coloured hair. Once out of sight of the circling grove of yew trees, she leapt lightly through the familiar, frosty undergrowth, picking her way through the woods to the little woven bower of willow wands that she had made secretly during the day. She took off her woollen girdle and wove it in and out, back and forth, until it became part of the bower, then from inside her kirtle she pulled a tiny straw plaited doll. She pushed it between one of the loops that her twisted girdle formed, so that it was held there firmly and bobbed up and down in the breeze. Then she sat back on her heels and solemnly chanted:

> 'Brig, Brig, bring us a bairn.
> Bonny as flowers.

Bright as the day.
Brave as a wolf.'

Magda sat there for a while, watching the Biddy doll bounce up and down, and she sighed. Many a woman, both young and old, would be doing the same thing this night, warm by their hearths. But Magda felt that she must do it shamefully in secret. She could not explain to Marian the great wish she had for a child. The Forestwife would be full of sensible, practical objections.

'You're too young! We're so busy! Haven't you got enough to do, helping me with all the suffering folk that come here to the clearing? Anyway, wishes never do come true in the way you want them to!'

Magda pushed these nagging doubts away as she pulled her girdle carefully out of the bower and fastened it around her waist once more. However foolish Marian might think her still the young woman's spirits rose, for the woods were full of sweet scents and magical mists. On Brig's Night the year was young and fresh, and on such a night Magda could believe that her wish might be granted.

When Magda got back to the cottage Marian was outside, holding up a lantern and talking in a low urgent voice to two strangers. The chickens and geese fussed and honked at the interruption to their sleep. Cats circled about the newcomers, waving their tails, greeting them with curiosity and suspicion. The smoking lantern gave enough flickering light to show a poor woman, her face contorted with pain, far gone in labour, a pale girl-child beside her, trembling with fear.

'Ah Magda,' Marian spoke with relief at her return. 'I need you. These two met a giant of a man whilst wandering in the woods, so they say. They were very fearful, but instead of harming them, he sent them here.'

Magda laughed. 'Aye. That would be John, my father,' she said.

Marian smiled for a moment, but she was too concerned for the plight of the woman to spend more time teasing. 'Here Magda, take this bairn will you and feed her. Take her through to the lean-to and find bedding.'

Magda nodded. She reached up to the shelf for the stone pitcher that they saved the goats milk in, and took a hunk of grainy bread from beside the hearth stone. This was a common enough situation and Magda was well used to sorting out frightened children.

She lit a rush-light from Marian's lantern. 'Follow me!' she told the girl, then headed through to the lean-to. They were greeted by much friendly bleating from the few goats that had been spared for the winter and now slept warm in amongst the straw.

Though the girl's hands still shook she ate hungrily, dipping sops of bread into the warm goat's milk. Magda scraped together a pile of straw and made a sleeping place with the rugs that they kept there.

'Now, settle down for the night,' Magda told her when she'd finished eating. 'Your mother will be well taken care of.'

The girl lay down obediently, but though exhausted, she lay on the bundled straw restless and wide-eyed.

'Can't you sleep?' Magda asked, after a while.

The girl shook her head.

'I'll sleep here with you,' Magda said, thinking practically that she might as well stay there for the night as her own pallet by the hearthstone must surely be taken by the labouring mother. She made another straw pile and sank down onto it with a sigh.

'Don't fear,' she said to the girl. 'All will be well.' Magda lay back and smiled to herself. It seemed to her almost as though Brig had answered her prayer immediately, but as Marian always said not quite in the way that she'd hoped for. 'Ah Brig,' she muttered to herself. 'I asked for a bairn and you sent me a strange little lass and a babe arriving soon.' Then she spoke more loudly to the girl. 'What do they call you, honey?'

The child stared up at her with large, dark, fearful eyes. Then suddenly she seemed to muster her courage and spoke with dignity. 'My name is Brigit,' she said.

'Oh!' Magda gasped, her heart thundering, for a moment. 'How strange! You are Brigit, and you come here to us on Brig's Night.' Then she told herself not to be stupid. There were many young girls named Brigit for the popular Christian Saint who'd once lived in Ireland and whose feast day came at the beginning of February. But others whispered that Brig's Night was much older than Christianity and brought a magic more ancient, belonging to the fierce goddess Brigantia whose people had lived here, long ago.

Magda blew out the rush-light but sensed that Brigit, though still now and silent beside her, lay wide awake. 'What a strange lass,' she told herself. 'Why cannot I be content with things as they are? What have I brought here? What have I wished for now?'

The next morning found Magda hard at work in the clearing, bending and pegging down the tips of the lowest branches on one of the great yews. She hammered the pegs firmly into dry ground, making a meagre hut that would shelter the poor mother and her two children for a little while once the ordeal of birth was safely over.

Brigit dragged spindly willow branches towards her from the woods, while animal-like bellows came from the hut. The girl looked anxiously up at Magda but said nothing.

'Don't fear,' Magda told her cheerfully. 'The bairn will soon be born, and then you shall have a new brother or sister. Marian, the Forestwife is the best midwife in Barnsdale.'

Magda spoke with a confidence she did not quite feel. It was true that nobody knew more about birthing than Marian, but this labour was going on for a long time, far too long. The mother must be growing exhausted.

The girl's eyes suddenly swam with tears. 'Aye,' she whispered at last. 'But I think the bairn should have been born by now, and . . . my father should be here.'

'Aye. So he should,' Magda agreed. 'Where is the man?'

The girl hiccuped, and swallowed hard. 'In Nottingham Jail. He's sent there for breaking the Forest Laws. We fear

7

he'll die before they try him.' Once released, tears now flowed fast down her cheeks, as she sobbed out her worst fears. 'And . . . and when they do try him, well, we cannot pay the fine. There is nowt for him but to lose fingers, or maybe an eye, and I cannot bear to think of my father blinded.'

Magda dropped the branch that she held and went to fling her arms about the child. She spoke through gritted teeth, with quiet anger. 'There's not many that can pay the Forest Court's high fines! This new Sheriff puts them up every month.'.

'All Father did was take a hare!' Brigit cried.

'Damn this evil king and his Forest Laws,' Magda growled. 'We hear now that he's taken another stretch of waste, north of Langden, and turned it into Royal Hunting Forest. He gets rid of the old Sheriff, who was nought but a buffoon and brings in this new man, de Rue, who's utterly ruthless in his duty and carries not a drop of compassion in his blood.'

'Aye, they all fear him,' Brigit agreed.

'The fines go to pay for great gangs of mercenaries.' Now Magda was in full spate there was no stopping her. 'We call them his wolfpacks. The king turns the very food in our mouths and the earth beneath our feet to money for his wars!' She spat on the ground, then spoke more gently seeing that her anger did nought to help the child's misery. 'But we are your friends Brigit, and we will not let you or your mother starve. Your father is not the only one to go hunting in Sherwood. If my father had a pound for every hare he'd taken, he'd be a rich man.'

'Your father breaks the Forest Laws too?' Brigit gasped.

'Every day of his life, honey,' Magda laughed.

Despite her fears, the girl could not hold back her curiosity about these strange woodland folk. 'Is the Forest-wife your mother?' she asked.

Brigit and her mother had struggled fearfully through the wastes, knowing only the frightening stories that they'd heard of a witchlike woman called the Forestwife, who lived hidden magically away in the deepest part of Barnsdale with the wild Hooded One, the wolf-man, who was her companion.

Magda smiled at the question. 'The Forestwife is not the mother I was born to,' she said. 'My mother died when I was a babe. Marian has mothered me ever since, but my father is that giant fellow John. The one who sent you here from Sherwood.'

Brigit's eyes opened wide. 'They say that he walks with the Hooded One, along with the rebel monk whose fierce hound catches arrows and snaps them in its mouth!'

Magda laughed. 'Aye, all that is true, but believe me, you've nowt to fear from them. Now you forget about those wicked outlaw fellows for a while, for we must get this shelter made. We'll weave the willow in and out of the yew branches and lay turfs of grass on the top. Then there'll be a dry, sweet-smelling hut, all ready when your mother comes from the Forestwife's cottage with a fine new babe in her arms.'

More grunts and moans could be heard, but Magda ignored the sounds of pain and made Brigit work even harder. They were almost finished and laying rushes on

9

the floor of the makeshift shelter when the sound of a galloping horse frightened the girl.

Magda stopped for a moment to listen, a warning finger to her lips. The thundering of the hooves ceased and a peculiar stamping rhythm followed. Magda's stern face broke into a smile.

'Don't fear,' she shook her head. 'It's my sweetheart Tom on his fine horse Rambler. I swear he loves that horse as much as me! He's slowed up now and he's finding his way through the secret maze of paths that keeps our clearing safe and hidden.'

They came out from the new shelter as a grey stallion entered the clearing. Tom was a tall fair-haired man, older than Magda, who rode as though he'd been born on horseback. Hanging over the horse's rump was a large, dead stag, a fallow deer from the Royal Hunting Forest of Sherwood.

'You see,' Magda told Brigit, pointing to the beast. 'I told you your father was not alone in breaking the laws.'

2

The Bishop of Hereford

Tom swung down from the saddle and hugged Magda. Brigit smiled shyly while they kissed passionately. As Tom led his horse towards the Forestwife's cottage, she saw that his left leg dragged a little.

'What is it? Why do you look so pleased?' Magda asked.

'His Grace the Bishop of Hereford comes visiting!'

'What here? Visiting us?'

'Aye. Robert and John are bringing him, and his men. They follow close behind with Brother James.'

Magda was shocked. 'Here to our secret place?'

Tom laughed. 'That's why I fetch this beast. We shall dine on roast venison.'

'You must be mad to feed a bishop on the King's deer?'

Tom shook his head. 'This bishop will not blink at it. He will delight in it.'

Suddenly Magda remembered the birthing. She grabbed Tom's arm and pulled him back, away from the cottage. 'Stop! We must wait! Marian will not thank us for bothering her just now. There's a child coming into its life.' She nodded at the watchful girl behind her.

Tom stopped obediently but the eager look would not leave his face. 'This is the Bishop of Hereford,' he began. 'He's no supporter of the king.'

But Magda would not listen.

'Since when do we feast with bishops?' she cried. 'What does Robert think he's doing?'

Tom laughed and kissed her nose. 'We meant to rob him; you know how Robert teases these rich travellers. He found great bags of gold on the pack-mules in the bishop's train, and swore he'd invite the bishop to dine, then make him pay for it. But then we discovered the man's name, and reason he rides south with such a great store of gold!'

Brigit tugged at Magda's arm. 'More horses,' she cried, excitement overcoming her fear. 'Your father the giant, a hooded man and the monk – there's the monk with his famous dog!'

Then into the clearing strode Robert, the close-fitting hood that he always wore fastened tight about his cheeks, hiding the deep scar that ran from ear to chin, stout Brother James followed them, his dog Fetcher leaping at his heels. Magda ran to hug her father. Robert led a huge fine-decked stallion, a tall man with white close-cropped hair astride. The visitor was clad in good leather riding breeks and boots, and a fine purple cloak, a gold cross hung about his neck; they were followed by twenty men at arms, more pack-horses and a wagon.

'Grand visitors for you daughter,' cried John, stooping low to give Magda a kiss.

'Marian!' Robert bellowed, pleased as could be. 'Come out and see who I've brought. Here's His Grace the Bishop of Hereford wishes to meet the Forestwife.'

'She's busy,' Magda hissed.

But the woven curtain that covered the doorway to the cottage was thrown aside. Marian came from the shadows into the light, her face pale, grey flecked hair ruffled, her apron soaked with fresh blood. In her arms she carried a tiny newly born child. She blinked at Robert stupidly, then looked past him to the bishop who still sat astride his horse.

'Forgive us Your Grace,' she spoke quietly. 'It's not the best time for visitors. This babe has had a struggle to be born, and his mother has just lost her life.'

There was a moment of silence then a small hiccuping sob came from Brigit. 'You said . . . y-you said the Forest-wife would save her.'

'I did believe she would.' Magda turned slowly, her face full of sorrow, and went to gather the distressed child into her arms.

Wearily Marian set about cleaning herself and organising a feast. She sent Tom to beg help from their friends who lived close by. Philippa the blacksmith's wife and Lady Isabel came from Langden Manor. With them came Will Stoutley, Robert's friend, who'd gone to work as Langden's reeve when the old Lady Matilda died and Isabel became Lady of the Manor in her own right. They also brought

13

a strong young mother who was willing to feed the newly born babe along with her own.

Mother Veronica and Sister Rosamund came from their woodland convent where they lived as the Sisters of the Magdalen, and Gerta the old besom-maker, who lived close by with her three young grandsons. They all brought food and drink to swell the feast and soon the clearing was thronging with bustle and work.

John and Brother James butchered the deer, fixed up a spit and got fires going for roasting. A trestle table was set close to the fire as the evening turned chill. They worked fast together, for Robert was in the habit of bringing unexpected visitors to dine. Though never before had he brought anyone as rich and powerful as the Bishop of Hereford; Robert usually had quite a different way of dealing with bishops!

Magda took no part in the preparations but sat in the small shelter with Brigit, trying to give what little comfort she could, talking and soothing until the child at last fell exhausted to sleep. Marian busied herself with washing and wrapping the new babe, and then with food preparations, ignoring Robert and the bishop. Indeed the two men were soon so deep in conversation that no courteous words of ceremony or welcome seemed needed. They spoke together in low urgent voices and Marian recognised the note of quiet excitement in Robert. She knew it only too well.

'What does this mean?' she asked herself. 'What wild scheme are we in for now?'

*

It was only when the meat was cooked and served with trenchers of fresh baked bread that Marian sat down and spoke to their guest.

'Humble food, Your Grace,' she said. 'But fresh and wholesome.'

The Bishop shook his head dismissing her worries. 'I eat very little,' he said.

Marian could believe that; the man was thin as a willow wand. At least he was no pampered overfed lover of luxury as so many of the bishops seemed to be.

'Marian,' Robert stood up formally and bowed to the Bishop. 'Let me present to you His Grace the Bishop of Hereford, Giles de Braose.'

Marian gasped and stared at the Bishop with new interest. 'De Braose? Did you say de Braose?'

Brother James laughed at her surprise. 'We thought that would interest you.'

'Are you . . .?' Marian faltered. 'Are you?'

An expression of pain touched the Bishop's face, and he nodded. 'I am the brother of William who died an exile in France. Matilda de Braose was my very dear sister-in-law, and well—' the Bishop clenched his jaw. 'You know what happened to her, and my poor nephew.'

There was a moment of quiet. All the forest folk knew only too well how the King had persecuted the de Braose family. He'd taken Matilda prisoner along with her son and it was whispered fearfully throughout the country that he'd starved them to death.

'Did the King's quarrel touch you . . . er, Your Grace?' Philippa asked, curiosity getting the better of courtesy.

Giles de Braose swallowed hard, looking round at all their serious faces. He seemed touched by their concern but Marian got the impression of a man who rarely let his feelings show.

'Me? I fled to France, but the king has invited me back and reinstated me. The fool thinks that I have forgiven him.' A wry smile touched the corners of his mouth. 'Now I travel the Great North Road from Helmsley Castle, where Robert de Ros gathers together an army of northerners. The gold I carry will buy weapons and fighting men for those who support us in the South. We shall bring out our charter, the one that is true to the laws King Henry made, and demand that the King reinstate his father's rule, and begin to deal justly with this country. If he will not, then believe me, his days are numbered, and at last my family shall be revenged.'

Marian nodded her head. Now it all became clear. There had been many whispers from those who passed through Barnsdale that even the most powerful northern barons were tired of King John's constant demands. He invented new fines and taxes every day, funding battles on foreign soil that were meaningless to all but him. So now, at last, rebellion was truly in the air.

The Bishop's men ate heartily of the King's deer, but the Bishop took little food. The outlaws ate quietly, with restraint, thoughtful at the Bishop's news.

Robert was fired with excitement. 'We could muster a hundred archers,' he suggested. 'Poor men, ill-fed and ragged, but greatly skilled with the bow and they are full of bitter resentment and hungry for change.'

The Bishop looked stunned for a moment but then he accepted this offer of support, though it came from so strange a quarter. 'Such men would be of value. I shall send word to you,' he promised. 'As soon as we are ready to move.'

'We'll come at once,' Robert assured him. 'We'll march to join you, travelling day and night.'

Marian looked from the Bishop to the outlaw, uneasy at this willingness for battle. Though so different in their stations in life, yet still they were two of a kind. The same fanatical gleam was there in the eyes.

As the evening air turned cold Marian got up and taking a flaming brand from the fire she went to the newly built hut. Magda was sitting shivering on the floor with her arms wrapped about Brigit. The girl's face was puffy and tearstained, but she slept.

'I think we should bring her out to the fire now,' Marian told her. 'Even though it means waking her, we must warm you both and make her eat and drink.'

Magda moved gently so that the child began to wake. 'Come, wake up now, sleepy one,' she spoke softly. Then her tone changed and she asked angrily, nodding at the Bishop. 'What is he doing here?'

Marian sighed. 'He is Giles de Braose, brother-in-law to the great Matilda that the King starved to death.'

Magda's eyes opened very wide. 'The one who was locked up with her son and neither of them seen again?'

Marian nodded. 'This man fled to France, but now he's

back and, believe me, he is bent on vengeance. Now do you understand?'

'Oh yes,' said Magda. 'Yes, I do.' Then she turned to Brigit, who was stirring, and starting to shiver. 'Come on, poor lass,' she whispered. 'Time to warm you up and fill your belly.'

At last the girl woke properly. 'My mother?' she murmured.

'I fear that is true sweetheart. Your mother has gone, but now you must eat and drink and warm yourself, for you must go on living.' Magda pulled her to her feet and led her firmly towards the fire.

Brigit was made to eat. She was too tired and miserable to argue and sat quietly nibbling at the food and warming her hands. Magda left her in Marian's care and went to sit between her father and Tom. He rubbed her back and shoulders. 'You're freezing Magda,' he said.

The Bishop watched Marian as she fed the young girl who shivered and wept, but obediently accepted the food. 'This child,' he asked. 'She is the daughter of the poor woman who died and sister to that new-born child?'

Marian nodded.

'Has she no father?' he asked.

'Aye, she has, but . . . ' Marian explained the man's plight. 'There is no money to pay his fine, and like so many he rots in Nottingham Jail.'

'That is one thing that the barons will demand of the King,' the Bishop said. 'We shall put this wicked ruler into a state of fear and demand removal of the Forest Laws.'

Marian looked across at Robert, and stopped feeding Brigit for a moment, spoon in hand. Everyone turned quiet at the sound of the Bishop's words. An expression of hope was there, just for an instant, on every face gathered about the flickering firelight.

'Now that,' said Marian quietly, 'would really mean something to us. That would truly be something worth fighting for.'

The Bishop waved one of his men forward and whispered in his ear. The man at once took a purse from his belt and gave it to his master. 'The barons can spare a little of their gold to pay one man's fine,' he said. 'Who will take this purse to Nottingham and fetch the child her father back?'

Everyone smiled and some clapped. 'I will take it Your Grace,' said Tom willingly.

Brigit looked up puzzled as the purse was passed from hand to hand.

'What are they doing?' she asked.

Marian took her hand. 'I believe they are going to get your father back for you,' she said.

The Bishop and his men rode out of the clearing early next morning with Robert, and James to set them on their way. Tom went along with them on Rambler, travelling as far as Nottingham, the Bishop's purse hidden in his jerkin.

Magda was soon at her most hated job, digging a rubbish pit, for the Bishop's overnight stay had left the clearing littered with chewed bones and soiled rushes. She insisted that Brigit should help her. 'It'll take her mind off the waiting,' she said.

Marian agreed, but towards noon she came to take Brigit to one side. 'How old are you, honey?' she asked.

'I'm twelve,' Brigit told her solemnly.

Marian sighed. 'Old enough for sorrow,' she said. 'Old enough to know your mind. Come with me.'

She led Brigit towards the cottage, but when the girl understood where they were going she pulled back, knowing that her mother's body still lay inside. Marian put her arm around the girl's shoulders. 'You do not have to go in,' she said. 'You do not have to look at her, but you may feel better if you do. There is naught that is fearful to see.'

Brigit trembled and could not speak.

'Do you wish to see your mother, child?'

'Yes,' she whispered.

'Come then.' Marian took her by the hand and led her inside.

What the Forestwife had said was true. There was nothing to fear. Old Gerta had washed the mother's body and combed her hair. She'd covered her with a clean soft woollen cloak and set a small, sweet scented posy of snowdrops in the work-roughened hands. The care-worn face was smoothed into an expression of peaceful rest.

Brigit knelt down and gently stroked her mother's hair.

Marian looked across at Gerta and tears filled both the women's eyes to see the young girl's touching gesture. Though they were constantly faced with pain and suffering, it never ceased to hurt. Marian dashed away the tears and forced herself to be practical. 'We cannot leave your mother unburied. We do not know how many days it will be before Tom can bring your father back. We could carry her to the Sisters of the Magdalen. They would give her a Christian burial in their churchyard, or we may bury her here at the top of the clearing where past Forestwives sleep beneath the yew trees. You must tell us what you want.'

Brigit shook her head. 'I cannot think,' she said.

Gerta got up and put her arm about the girl's shoulders. 'Would you like Marian to show you the place?'

'Aye,' Brigit allowed herself to be led back outside.

At the top of the clearing between two ancient yews there lay a row of unmarked graves, humps in the ground.

'It's very quiet here,' the girl whispered.

Marian nodded. 'We believe this clearing to be an ancient place of healing, with its circle of yews and magical warm spring. We do not know how old it is, but for as long as any of us can remember there has been a Forestwife living here; someone who will give help to any who come seeking it and do her best to heal.'

'We thought you a witch,' Brigit said, shamed at their foolishness. 'And we were fearful, but I am not feared of you now.'

Marian smiled. 'I am but a woman. I sometimes wish I were a witch, if such magic would give me better skills. I would have given anything to have saved your mother for you.'

'I know that you tried,' Brigit spoke with surprising maturity. 'I know that you did your best. Are these the graves of the ancient Forestwives?'

'Yes, but not only them. This one was Agnes, the old Forestwife and my dear nurse; she was also Robert's mother. This was Emma, my sweetest friend and Magda's mother. This one with still fresh earth is my own mother, Eleanor. The forest folk called her the Old One. It's just two months since I came home to find she'd died.'

22

'Did you feel all dull and tight inside you?' Brigit touched her chest.

'Aye,' Marian said. 'I did feel that, but it's slowly getting better. That morning, before I knew she'd died, I saw a she-wolf out in the woods. When I got back and found my mother gone, I thought the she-wolf had been my mother's spirit and I was so glad that I'd seen her going bravely on her way.'

Brigit nodded. 'This is a good place,' she said. 'My mother used to make herb medicines for the village folk – she'd like this place. Will you bury my mother here?'

Robert and James returned, noisy and energetic with their plans. 'We'll send word to all our friends. We'll muster every man we know.' Robert told Marian. 'Philippa's blacksmith husband is willing, and Rowan, too. Philippa says she is going, for she's determined not to lose her youngest son, and she says they'll need someone sensible to keep an eye on them! Isabel agrees that Will may go though she says she doesn't know how she'll manage without him. What about you, sweetheart? We'll be in desperate need of a healer. You were never far behind when it came to a fight!'

But Marian shook her head. 'I have bad feelings about it all,' she said. 'Though Giles de Braose seems to be an honourable man, I do not trust the other barons. Since when have they helped such as us? Besides, there must be a Forestwife here.'

As soon as Magda finished filling in the rubbish pit, Marian asked her to start digging the grave.

'Am I the only one around here who can wield a shovel?'
she complained. 'Ask my father, he that is so big and
strong. He's getting fat, he needs the exercise!'

John came to her laughing. They wrestled over the
shovel. 'Give it to me then daughter. I'll show you how
it's done.' Then suddenly their laughter died as they saw
Brigit watching them.

'I should like to dig my mother's grave,' she said
solemnly.

'Come little one,' said John quietly taking her hand.
'We'll all help, and do the job together.'

They assembled to bury the poor mother as dusk fell.
The young wet-nurse came over from Langden to join
them at the graveside, her own big babe on one hip and
the tiny child cradled in her other arm. The older child
wriggled about and the new-born babe began to cry. Both
Magda and Marian moved to help, but then stood back
as Brigit strode over to the woman and took her brother
into her arms. She rocked the child gently and stuck
her little finger into his mouth. The child was instantly
soothed.

Magda and Marian looked at each other. 'How old is
she?' Magda whispered.

'Older than her years,' Marian quietly replied.

'Sorrow can do that to young folk,' Gerta agreed.

Magda went to stand beside Brigit. 'Your new brother
should be named,' she said. 'You are his sister. You should
be the one to name him.'

Brigit looked uncertain for a moment but then smiled

down at the baby's soft patch of hair. 'My father is called Peter,' she said. 'I shall call my brother Peterkin for him.'

'Peterkin is a fine name,' Magda touched the baby's cheek.

The days that followed were full of bustle, and the Forest-wife's clearing was filled with the smell of hot metal poured to make arrowheads. The scrape of knife on wood could be heard as they worked hard to finish new strong bows. Arrows went whistling towards their targets, for Robert had all who presented themselves willing at bow practice each day.

Gerta's three grandsons begged to join the older men but the old woman was adamant that they were far too young and she marched them away, back to their small home in the woods, so that they shouldn't be tempted further by watching the preparations. Philippa and her husband were to go with Isabel's blessing, for their skills as blacksmiths would be needed as much as those willing to fight.

'Promise me you'll stay out of the battle?' Marian begged her friend.

Philippa had sighed. 'Oh aye,' she said. 'There'll be plenty to do without fighting. I dare say they'll have me hammering the dints from their swords and straightening crumpled arrowheads. They'll want their wounds tending, and they'll all need feeding. Trust me, I won't be joining any battle.'

'I don't trust you, any more than I trust Robert,' said

Marian, hugging her tightly. 'Just make sure you come back safely to us.'

Magda was excited by all the plans and action that surrounded her home. She spoke of going with the men but John would not agree to it. A happy relief from the war-like plans came when Tom brought back Brigit's father safe and well from Nottingham Jail. Brigit was overjoyed to see him but her happiness did not last long for the man was determined to join the rebels.

'But father we need you, me and little Peterkin,' she told him.

'Do you feel safe here with the Forestwife?' he asked.

'Yes,' she agreed.

'Please try to understand. I must go to fight against these wicked Forest Laws. They make our lives a misery.'

Brigit just stared at him, deep sadness in her eyes.

When Magda spoke again of going to fight, Tom silenced her by pointing to Brigit. 'She needs you my love,' he said. 'More than ever now that her father insists on coming.'

Soon after Easter one of the Bishop of Hereford's men rode into the clearing with news that the barons were gathering at Northampton. Brigit's father was amongst those that set off, prepared for battle, all following the Hooded One.

4

Gerta's Grandsons

Though the clearing felt quiet after the army of rebel northeners had gone, there was plenty to do as always. The May Day celebrations were meagre compared with the usual wild feast and dancing that went on, but they didn't let the day go by in silence.

'Who can be our Green Man this year?' Magda wondered. ''Tis quite a problem, now that all our men are gone.'

''Twould be good to make young Brigit our May Queen,' Marian, suggested. 'The child is so solemn and forlorn.'

'Ah yes!' Magda agreed. 'The honour would do her good and maybe cheer her and that gives me an idea; a very young Green Man would be just right to dance with Brigit.'

She persuaded Davy, the youngest of Gerta's grandson's, to allow them to paint his cheeks with green woodland dyes and cover his hair and clothes in fresh green leaves. When the misty May morning arrived, Davy came

27

dancing out from the woodland as the Green Man, bringing the summer in as the sun rose high in the sky. He enjoyed his part and delighted in crowning the surprised Brigit with a garland of sweet hawthorn blossom to make her his Green Lady, and the beautiful May Queen. The older women clapped and sang with determined cheerfulness as the children danced around the maypole by the trysting tree.

As the weather grew warmer, small scraps of news from the rebels reached the Forestwife's clearing and they were grateful for the messages brought by Isabel, whose Manor of Langden, lay closer to the Great North Road. Within weeks they heard that the rebels had attacked the King's stronghold at Northampton, while the King stayed near to Oxford, gathering his wolfpack about him. Then the northeners marched on to London, climbing the walls and opening the city gates on a Sunday while the good townsfolk were at mass. They set about besieging the Tower of London.

'Sounds like Robert,' said Magda. 'If it's not his idea, he'll certainly be enjoying himself.'

'Aye,' Marian agreed with a sigh.

'There's some still loyal to the crown,' Isabel told them. 'Nichola la Haye holds Lincoln Castle for the King.'

Marian's mouth dropped open in surprise. 'Nichola . . . the constable's wife. Isn't she a frail old woman? What of her husband?'

Isabel laughed. 'She's old, but I doubt you'd call her frail! Her husband was from home when rebels sur-

28

rounded Lincoln. They thought they'd take it with ease, but they were wrong. It seems Nichola set about defending the place like a veteran warrior, and they've not moved her.'

'I can't help thinking, good for her!' cried Magda. 'But she's on the wrong side!'

'Yes,' Isabel agreed. 'We should have such a woman organising *our* men!'

Marian shook her head. 'I fear for our men,' she said. 'I don't trust these bishops and barons; I'm sure they're after their own gains. There are no clear sides to this struggle.'

As the weather grew warm and the June buds burst filling the woodland with lush green leaves they heard the most wonderful news. The King was asking for peace and agreeing to meet the rebels at Runnymede, promising he'd give them their charter. While the barons and bishops swore fealty once more to King John, the rebel army feasted.

A smaller celebration took place deep in Barnsdale Woods. The nuns brought bread and ale, Isabel ordered some of her geese slaughtered, and Marian cut down the haunch of venison that had been smoking above her cooking fire for weeks. Magda took young Brigit out into the woods and taught her how to snare rabbits.

The meal they produced was magnificent by their standards. The woodland folk sang, danced and drank, toasting the hoped-for lifting of the Forest Laws. Some of the young boys got a little too bold with drink and staggered off in the direction of Sherwood, swearing that they'd tear the fences down, and let out the deer.

Their mothers were fearful at the idea, but Magda was scornful. 'They'll be in no fit state to tear anything down. They'll end up snoring in a ditch.'

The Forestwife and her friends slept late the next morning. As they rose and began to set everything to rights, some of the lads came stumbling back through the clearing, weak-legged, sick and dazed. Marian made them drink a mug of steaming herb tea, sweetened with honey, while Magda gave them a good telling off.

'Serves you right,' she snapped. 'Puking up like little pigs! What a waste of good barley ale! I hope you have thudding heads all day!'

'We all have to learn,' Marian told them, smiling. 'I seem to remember a little lass that performed a wild dance one May Day feast. Then fell over and had to be carried sick and weeping to her pallet.'

'Hmm!' Magda, frowned. 'It was the dancing that made me sick not the drink!'

Brigit swept up dutifully around their feet, saying nothing, but listening and watching, taking everything in.

When the sun was high in the sky, the lads were sent home to stop their mothers from worrying. 'Fresh air and a good fast walk through the woods!' Magda told them. 'That's what you lot need!'

Dusk was falling when Gerta came back into the clearing, her face all creased with worry.

'What is it Gerta?' Magda asked. 'Have those grandsons of yours still got thick heads?'

'Thick heads or not, I don't know. I've not seen them all day,' said Gerta angrily. 'Our Jack swore he'd mend the fencing on our close, for my grey gander keeps escaping. When those lads get back I'll wring their necks. I wondered if you'd seen them?'

Magda shook her head. 'No, I've not seen your lads, but I shouldn't fret,' she soothed. 'They'll be sleeping it off under some hedge. We've had some of their barley-brained comrades here. Marian dosed them for their pains, but we've not seen your three.'

Gerta folded her arms and shook her head. She looked exhausted. 'I've asked all their friends,' she insisted. 'I've been walking round the woods since noon. All they can tell me is that my lads *did* go off towards Sherwood with axes stuck in their belts.'

Magda began to feel uneasy. Gerta was much loved in Barnsdale, for despite being old and poor, she'd taken her three young grandsons to live with her when their parents both died of the fever. She'd struggled to raise them on her pitiful earnings in her small hut close to Langden. Gerta loved the three boys fiercely and, though she was getting bent and thin with age, she usually kept them well disciplined with the sheer force of her temper.

'Axes in their belts?' Magda muttered. The picture that came into her mind of the three lads marching towards Sherwood brought a chilling touch of anxiety. 'I'll fetch Marian and see what she thinks,' she said.

Marian came out from the cottage followed by Brigit;

she was immediately concerned. 'Towards Sherwood?' she confirmed. 'With axes?'

They made Gerta sit down and without being told, Brigit brought out a warm drink for the old woman. Marian bent and sniffed the brew. 'Camomile,' she said. 'Well chosen, lass.'

'Soothes anxiety,' the girl told her solemnly. 'So mother always said.'

They stood quietly, watching the old woman sip the brew. Marian did not want to make Gerta more fearful, but she was filled with foreboding. The sound of a horse clopping through the darkening woods made them even more worried, but it was Isabel who rode into the clearing. She swung down from her sturdy grey mare and they saw from her face that she had something bad to tell them.

'What now?' whispered Marian.

Isabel would not speak straight out. She sat down beside Gerta and took hold of her hand, then began speaking gently, hating the news that she brought. 'There's three young lads been caught chopping down palings on the edge of Sherwood.'

'No!' Gerta cried.

Isabel nodded. 'I fear so. Hundreds of deer are loosed, and the verderers furious. The new Sheriff de Rue, has sent word, they're to be hanged.'

'Ah no!' Gerta cried again.

Magda gasped. Brigit's hands shook as she took the cup back from Gerta; only Marian was stony-faced.

'Not my lads?' Gerta whispered. The old woman started

rocking backwards and forwards while Magda sat down on her other side and tried to comfort her.

Isabel's face twisted with pity. 'There's more, but I don't know whether to say it!'

Gerta stopped rocking at once. 'Tell me!' she demanded. 'I have to know!'

'The three will not give their names, but the oldest is a tall dark haired lad and the youngest fair and nowt but a child.'

'My Davy! They cannot hang my Davy. He's only eleven years old!'

'If my father and Robert were here,' Magda growled. 'If only Tom were here.'

'Well, they are not,' said Marian angrily. 'They have gone off on a wild goose chase. What fools we've all been! How could we think the King would end the Forest Laws just like that?' She snapped her fingers hard. Then she took a deep breath and sighed. 'Well, our men are not here, so we must take action ourselves.'

'Aye,' Isabel agreed. 'We must do something, but what? We must think hard and fast. The lads are due to hang tomorrow at noon at Ollerton Crossroads. The Sheriff himself will ride there to see it done.'

Marian frowned, tapping her head, racking her brains for an idea. Then she suddenly looked up. 'I'm asking myself, what would Robert do if he were here? And, I think I know.'

'Huh!' Magda snorted. 'He'd disguise himself in filthy rags. He'd dress himself as a potter, or a priest, or a tinker, and he'd go marching right up to the gibbet!'

33

'Exactly!' Marian agreed. 'And that is what we will do! We'll disguise ourselves and we shall go marching right up to the gibbet. But, I do not fancy filthy rags; I have a much more respectable idea. The boys live close to Langden, do they not? The Sisters of the Magdalen are Langden's nuns. Couldn't they insist on seeing them; to pray for their souls? Surely any man who refused such a request would fear his own soul damned!'

'Aye,' whispered Gerta, faintly hopeful. 'My hut's within the bounds of Langden Parish. The sisters would have the right to beg such a favour! But even if you managed to get them away, then the sisters would be followed and punished. We'd all be punished!'

'Yes,' said Isabel. 'But if we disguised ourselves as nuns and called ourselves by another name, not the Sisters of the Magdalen, then perhaps it could just work! It seems your brave lads will not admit they are from Langden, so the Sheriff doesn't know where they really come from. I think they mean to save us from trouble by keeping quiet. It might be just that courage that brings us the means to save them!'

'You could call yourselves St Bridget's Nuns,' Brigit suggested, her voice shrill with sudden excitement. 'There were St Bridget's nuns, who lived near Goldwell when I was a babe. Mother named me after them. But the last old nun died three years ago and now the convent stands a ruin in the woods.'

Marian hugged her. 'Clever lass!' she cried. 'It would sound real and even familiar, but if the Sheriff should send his men to hunt St Bridget's nuns, they'd find nothing, but a deserted convent.'

5

Ollerton Crossroads

Magda laughed. 'It seems we have our plan.'

'Yes, but we must speak with Mother Veronica,' said Isabel. 'I know she'll help

'I'll take my bow and arrow,' Magda cried. 'Though I never thought to see myself as a nun.'

'Yes,' Marian agreed, her cheeks flushed and eyes bright with anger. 'And I must go to Ollerton too. I do not like to leave the clearing without a Forestwife, but my shooting skills will be needed.'

'Shall I come with you?' Brigit whispered.

Magda shook her head smiling, touched by the offer. This quiet child was certainly no coward. 'She really is as brave as a wolf,' she murmured.

The hopes raised by their plan made Gerta calm and strong once more. 'No honey,' she told Brigit. 'You and I, little lass, we shall be Forestwife while Marian is away. I dare say we can manage well enough together, just for a while.'

Marian nodded. 'That is a good plan Gerta.' She unfas-

tened the beautiful woven girdle that she wore, the girdle
of the Forestwife, retying it carefully around the old
woman's thin waist. 'Take care of it,' she said. 'And any
who come seeking help.' She kissed them both, then
reached to take down her bow from the nail above the
small window.

'Get mine too,' Magda was eager to be off. 'I shall fetch
the new made arrows from the lean-to.'

'No,' Marian told her. 'There is something important
for you to do first. Ride with Isabel and fetch Mother
Veronica and Sister Rosamund? We need some real nuns,
if we are to be convincing and ask if we may borrow extra
veils and habits. Oh, and Isabel, I think we are going to
need more horses. Can you find us some?'

Magda and Isabel rode through the woods, obedient to
Marian's orders. 'I love her when she is like this,' Magda
cried. 'Suddenly she throws aside all her carefulness and
hurls herself into a wild adventure, all fired up.'

'Yes!' Isabel agreed, her face drawn with anxiety. 'But
what we plan is fraught with danger. Magda?' she said,
touching the young woman's arm. 'I do not forget how
you came with Marian to rescue me when the wolfpack
walled me up, leaving my mother and me to die. You
risked your lives to save us then, and now we all risk our
lives again for Gerta's lads. This is just as desperate and
fearful a thing to attempt!'

Three new-made gibbets stood on the old platform outside
the lock-up at Ollerton Crossroads. The Sheriff of Nottingham's men were busy stringing up nooses. The news

that there was to be a hanging had caused quite a stir so that the worn grass around the lock-up thronged with people. Some cheerfully elbowed their way through the crowd to get a good view of the spectacle, but many were moved to pity.

A skinny washerwoman pushing a handcart piled with dirty linen and small children spoke with sorrow. 'So young I hear. Nobbut bairns!'

'Does not this new charter change the law?' asked a stooped and aged alewife who carried her wares in buckets, fixed onto a wooden yoke across her shoulders. 'A hanging's good for business, but I thought the laws were to be changed.'

'Who knows what it does? Can laws change over night like that?'

'They say the Sheriff is making an example of them, won't let it go unpunished. He fears to have every young ruffian in the wastes ripping down palings if he shows mercy.'

'That man hasn't got a drop of mercy in his veins,' came the reply.

Others saw humour in the tragedy. 'Good on the lads,' an old man chuckled. 'They don't die for nowt. The King's deer run wild through Barnsdale and there's plenty with a full belly for once.'

'Aye,' the washerwoman laughed and dug him in the ribs. 'The scent of stewed venison reeks from every hut.'

Shortly before noon a plump, elderly nun came pushing

through the crowd towards the lock-up, followed by six of her sisters.

'Make way, make way! St Bridget's nuns from Goldwell,' Mother Veronica cried. 'These children live close to Goldwell Priory. We have travelled all morning, coming as soon as we heard. We must pray with them.'

The captain hesitated, uncertain as to whether he should allow this seemingly holy intrusion.

'Let us see the young sinners,' the Prioress begged. 'We must be sure that they repent. Should you deny this, why man, you'd risk your own immortal soul.'

The captain argued for a while, but his men shuffled anxiously and crossed themselves. At last he gave way and unlocked the door.

'Only for a moment,' he barked. 'The Sheriff will be here at noon!'

Mother Veronica marched into the darkness of the cramped room, her equally plump sisters crowding close behind her. There was a moment of confusion and hubbub, then the deep clear voice of Sister Rosamund could be heard chanting prayers for the dying.

Mother Veronica appeared again. 'Bless you for your mercy,' she cried making the sign of the cross.

The guards bowed their heads as nine nuns followed their prioress out, one of them very small and stumbling a little on the trailing skirt of the habit. In the pressing crowd it was difficult for the men to see that more nuns came out than had ever gone in. As the Captain turned to lock the heavy door, onlookers pressed close behind him trying to get a glimpse of the ill-fated lads.

Once they were out and through the crowd, the nuns walked fast towards a group of horses sheltering beneath a great oak nearby. Isabel of Langden, already mounted on her own grey mare, held the reins.

A sudden shout of anger was heard above the muttering crowd. 'Empty! Get after them. Unholy bitches! They've got the prisoners! They've taken them!'

The nuns picked up their skirts and ran towards Isabel. People milled about, arguing and pushing, unsure of what was happening, and uncertain as to whose side they should take. This unexpected turn of events was providing nearly as good a show for them as a hanging. The guards roared with fury, shoving folk aside, trying to follow their prisoners, swords drawn. The nuns leapt up onto their waiting horses with wonderful agility. Only aged Mother Veronica had to be hauled onto her mount. They set off galloping north, but two of the tallest nuns held their horses back, snatching up bows from their saddles. They pulled arrows from full quivers hidden beneath their long skirted habits and sent a hail of them flying towards the guards.

The men leapt back, too surprised to answer the attack with speed. Then Marian shouted as she wheeled her horse about. 'Tell your Sheriff this – he shall not hang children! So says the Hooded One.'

The whispered name of the Hooded One flew through the crowd and at once the soldiers found themselves impeded. Buckets of overturned ale made the ground slip beneath their feet, while old men on sticks and small children stumbled against the guards. They roared with anger, as they seemed to trip and tread in piles of soiled linen and clothing whichever way they turned.

The rescuers and rescued got back to Barnsdale exhausted but elated with their success. The nuns returned quickly to their convent and their prayers, cleaning the mud stained habits thoroughly, so that no sign or evidence remained. Gerta's grandsons clung to her as she hugged and berated them in turn.

'This calls for another celebration,' Magda suggested.

'No,' Marian told her dryly. ''Twas too much celebration that brought them close to death. We'll have no more for the moment.'

The boys swore tearfully, they'd never drink again.

Later that night, when everyone had gone to their homes, Marian and Magda sat by the fire, quiet and weary. Brigit pounded roots in a wooden bowl, talking excitedly for once. 'I boiled up purslane for a sick baby who'd eaten green apples, and pennyroyal for Freda's birth pains. Then after Gerta had cut the cord, I gave her a warm brew of century to sip. Did I do right?'

Marian smiled. 'I couldn't have done better myself.'

Magda chuckled. 'A great deal better than I could have done.'

Then she lifted her head, suddenly alert at the sound of a horse moving slowly towards them, winding its way through the secret paths. All at once it turned into the familiar stamping rhythm of Rambler's hooves. They jumped up, snatching the lantern, all tiredness forgotten, and ran outside. Tom came riding into the clearing with Brother James mounted behind him. John strode at their side, the faithful Fetcher lolloping after them.

'Now we've got to have a celebration,' Magda cried.

'We'll have a small one,' Marian agreed. Then she sighed. 'Where's Robert?'

The men were tired and dusty from their journey. They sported a good crop of cuts and bruises but were otherwise unharmed.

'You're solemn for men who've just won a charter from their King!' Magda cried.

'Aye,' Tom hugged her tightly, but still would not smile. 'We've got good reason to be solemn. There was little in the charter for the likes of us, most of it favoured the barons – no real changing of the Forest Laws. All the King did was to grudgingly consent to give back the newest stretches of land that he'd put under the Forest Laws. We didn't think much of that! But even that small gain didn't last. Now the King says that he revoke's the whole agreement!'

'What?' Magda cried.

'I knew it,' Marian shook her head.

'The King has gone straight back on his word,' James told them, grimly fondling Fetcher's rough ears. 'First he says he will, then he says he won't. He claims that he was forced to grant it, and that makes the charter unlawful. The man can wriggle out of any hole.'

'Aye.' John agreed. 'He's sent abroad for more mercenaries and the rebel barons look for men and arms once more. They'll be fighting again soon enough, you can bet on it, but we'll not be with them. It's clear to us now, the barons care nowt for Forest Laws or commonfolk, they just want power for themselves.'

Marian pressed her lips tightly together, to stop herself from spitting out, I told you so.

The men brought news of Philippa's husband, who'd stayed in London working at his blacksmith trade for the rebel lords. 'They promise great wealth in payment,' said Tom. 'Rowan has stayed to help his father, but we doubt they'll ever see their money.'

Marian waited until they were fed and warmed by the fire before she asked again. 'And where is Robert?'

John shook his head. 'He was with us this morning, but there was hell to pay as we passed near Ollerton. Great gangs of the Sheriff's men marched everywhere, armed to the teeth. A guard picked me out as fellow to the Hooded One, so we had to split and run. Will insisted that he go straight back to Langden, he's anxious to see that all is well with Isabel. Why do you all smile so slyly?' John touched his daughter's cheek.

The women told of the day's events.

The men laughed and applauded them, but Marian thought she caught an anxious glance passing between John and Brother James.

'What is it?' she demanded. 'I know there is something! Is he hurt?'

There was a moment of hesitation.

'He is hurt!' she said.

'He took a bash on the head from a huge rock,' James said at last. 'The king's men drag about these powerful

43

new stone-throwing machines that they call the *trebuchet*. There's many of our fellows have been stunned and many dead for they hurl great rocks with such a power.'

Magda shuddered at his words.

'They can bring down walls, and towers with the things,' John added. 'And if you are in the wrong place . . .? Well Robert was in the wrong place as usual, but Philippa's looking after him. She won't leave his side. Better bodyguard than a bear, is Philippa. We thought it best to draw the guards away from them.'

Marian frowned. This was so unlike Robert, who was always in the thick of things. 'He *can* walk?' she asked.

'Oh aye,' John agreed. 'Your man walks, talks, eats and drinks, but sometimes what he says is rubbish.'

'Huh!' Marian cried. 'He always did talk rubbish.'

John smiled and nodded but he added solemnly. 'He goes wandering off in the wrong direction, if you do not keep a tight hold of him.'

That really alarmed her. 'I don't like the sound of it,' she whispered.

After the others had fallen asleep, Marian lit her lantern from the embers and went out into the darkness of the woods.

6

'Who is it that you think you've caught?'

Marian's search was fruitless and just as dawn light filtered through the trees, she returned to the cottage and fell asleep, exhausted. By the time she eventually woke again Magda had made oatcakes and the men had cleaned themselves in the warm waters of the Forestwife's spring. James and Tom started cutting yew staves for new bows.

'Robert's still not here?' Marian asked. 'Nor Philippa?'

John shook his head. 'Don't fret. I'm going off to look for them. We hadn't time to make plans and I don't know which way they'll come. Philippa might head for her home in Langden.'

'I'll come too,' Marian insisted.

But before they had a chance to set off Brigit, who'd been fetching firewood, came running and pointing. 'Gerta's coming!' she cried. 'Gerta's coming with an old woman who can't walk properly. She leads her by the arm.'

Marian went towards them, ready to give aid as ever, but a shiver of doubt touched her as the they came closer. Was this not Philippa's dark red kirtle and worn hooded cloak? But the bent, stumbling soul who leaned on Gerta could not be Philippa, who still strode tall and straight-backed through the woods, although she had aged. 'Who is this, Gerta?' she asked.

'Prepare yourself,' Gerta whispered. 'I fear you'll be shocked.' Then she reached over and pulled back her companion's hood.

Marian was indeed deeply shocked. It was Robert, but a Robert that she had never known. He trembled and clung to Gerta's arm, his skin grey and sweaty. He stared up at Marian as though she were a stranger, mumbling words that made no sense.

Marian's stomach churned. Robert had been hurt many times before, indeed he was covered with scars that she had cleaned and healed, but no stinking wound or rotting flesh had ever seemed as terrible to her as this clinging weakness or the blankness in his eyes.

'I knew you'd be fearful,' Gerta reached out to touch her arm. 'But believe me, I've seen this before from a blow to the head, and still they may recover.'

'Aye,' Marian forced herself to be sensible. 'I've seen it too and you are right, some do get better. Rest and good feeding may do a world of good. Let us get him inside by the fire. Have you seen Philippa?'

'I have,' Gerta agreed, miserably.

They steered Robert into the cottage and settled him

onto a straw pallet. As Marian fed him sips of a calming fever mixture, Gerta told them what had happened.

'There's much to tell and no time to waste,' the old woman was very agitated. 'I was alone, for Isabel has given my lads work up at Langden. Your friend Philippa came knocking at my door early this morning with the Hooded One at her side. She almost carried the man. Oh, I pray I have done right!'

'Tell us,' John spoke gently.

Gerta told them how Philippa and Robert had been tracked by some of the Sheriff's men, right through Barnsdale. It seemed they'd recognised the much-wanted Hooded One and were bent on getting themselves a rich reward.

'As soon as I let them in, Philippa started tearing off her clothes,' Gerta told them. 'I thought she'd gone mad, but then I came to understand and I helped her. I couldn't think what else to do. We stripped off Robert's clothes and exchanged them with Philippa's, so that he looked like this, and Philippa, she's so tall and upright, she looked like the Hooded One.'

'She's mad!' Magda gasped, starting to understand.

'Trust her,' Marian agreed. 'She's put herself in terrible danger.'

'She told me to bring him to you,' Gerta cried. 'She swore the men would ignore two old women, if they thought they'd got the Hooded One holed up. And she was right. They took no notice, letting us pass. All they did was to creep a little closer to my hut.'

'We've got to go,' Marian cried.

'Aye,' John leapt to his feet, lifting down the bows from the nail that they hung on.

Magda stuck her head out of the door and shouted for Tom and James, who were still unaware of this latest trouble.

'You stay!' John told Marian. 'Leave it to us!'

'But Philippa?' she cried, torn between concern for her sick lover and her dearest friend. 'I can't stay here by the fire, when she's in such danger.'

'I can look after the man,' a small voice spoke up. They turned to Brigit uncertainly.

'And I can stay with the lass,' Gerta told them. 'We played Forestwife together yesterday, now we can do it again. You get off as fast as you can and see that brave and crazy woman safe.'

They did not argue anymore, but turned and ran, Tom leaping onto Rambler and leading the way.

Though they went fast through the woodland paths they slowed as they neared Gerta's hut, knowing that it wouldn't do to charge straight in. Tom got down from his horse and led Rambler quietly towards the small hut. Though at first all seemed quiet, the faint snorting and champing of bits and restless brush of hooves in the undergrowth told them what they needed to know.

There were six of the Sheriff's men creeping slowly towards Gerta's doorway, swords drawn. Two crouched down beneath Gerta's small window hole, though it was scarcely big enough for a child to escape through. The band of men were small in number, but well armed and excited at the prize they thought within their grasp. The reward offered for Robert the Wolveshead, also known as the Hooded One, went up at every court-leet. The new Sheriff would be grateful indeed, to any man who brought him back to Nottingham, dead or alive.

Marian and her friends had no sooner taken stock of the situation than they heard a low cough, followed by a sharp bang that sent clouds of rooks shooting from their nests. Then came the thumping sounds of a struggle and angry shouts. As Marian moved forwards she saw that they'd ripped aside the woven curtain and kicked over the low wattle hurdles that formed a close to keep in Gerta's geese. Now they hauled out a tall struggling figure dressed in Robert's forest-dyed hood and short kirtle. Their impulse was to rush forwards and snatch Philippa, but experience held them back, telling them that acting at the right moment was imperative. Meanwhile Gerta's grey gander made a good job of flying at the men's eyes, while his companions honked and flapped in panic.

'We've got him!' the men crowed, warding off the beating wings. Philippa continued to fight.

'Ah! Damned fellow's kicked my shins.'

'Dead or alive?' another shouted. 'Hang him! Run him through! Less trouble dead.'

'Aye, but will Sheriff pay more if he's alive?'

'Aye, maybe. Get him on a horse, and get him trussed.'

Philippa was bundled onto the nearest waiting horse.

'Now,' John whispered. 'Before they get moving.'

Without further discussion, Marian and her friends took up their bows, each notching an arrow. They crept silently forwards, forming a half-circle about the Sheriff's men. Tom quietly mounted Rambler and urged him slowly on behind them. So quietly did they move and so close in colour to their surroundings were the woodland dyes of their clothing that they had their targets well lined up before one of the men noticed them. The man was so shocked that he couldn't speak, only croak and point his sword.

'Give us back our friend,' John's voice rang out. 'Give us our friend and you shall keep your lives.'

'Give up the Hooded One?' one of the men growled. 'You must be mad!'

'Fools!' It was Philippa who spoke, her voice full of mocking laughter. 'Who is it that you think you've caught?' Suddenly she pulled up Robert's short kirtle, exposing a pair of very female breasts.

The men gaped; their mouths open, eyes wide with astonishment. Marian and Magda could not suppress small snorts of laughter, but Philippa did not waste her moment. She was down from the horse and racing towards her friends in an instant. Tom hauled her up onto Rambler, then turned to gallop fast away, leaving the others to deal with the sheriff's men.

It was hard to aim carefully whilst holding back laughter, but they somehow managed to send a hail of arrows flying towards the still stunned soldiers. The four who'd pulled Philippa from the hut were killed outright, while the two by the window shot off in the direction of their horses. Magda and John moved to follow them, but could not keep up once the men were mounted and away.

'Who is it that you think you've caught?'

'Don't worry,' Marian called. 'They'll not return here in a hurry.' She chuckled for a moment, then suddenly her laughter fled. She snatched the nearest deserted horse by the reins. 'I must get back to Robert,' she cried.

7

A Fine Little Herbwife

While Marian rode back to the clearing on the stolen horse, Magda, John and James took Gerta's digging tools and buried the four men secretly in the woods. They set about mending the smashed wattle hurdles, then caught the still squawking geese and returned them to the safety of their close once more. Then when all was neat and secure once more, they set off with three strong new horses for the Forestwife's clearing.

Philippa and Tom were just ahead of her when Marian arrived back at the cottage. The two women jumped down from their mounts and hugged each other fiercely.

'How could you?' Marian cried. 'Trust you to save yourself so rudely.'

'Well . . . it worked didn't it?' Philippa laughed shamelessly. 'There was no need for you to go rushing out there. I could have sorted out those fools myself!'

'I swear that's true,' said Tom, shaking his head and smiling. 'Philippa and the grey gander might have managed very well! But now, what of Robert?'

The joy fell from both women's faces, and they turned towards the cottage.

'How long has he been like this?' Marian asked.

'Almost a se'n night,' Philippa told her. 'He seemed to be improving, then slipped back worse than ever. I thought it best to bring him home to you.'

Marian stopped, smiling sadly. 'Aye, this is his home, though he never spends much time here. It is as much a home as he has ever known. Robert was born here in this clearing. Did you know?'

'Aye,' Philippa thrust her arm through her friend's. 'I remember his mother Agnes telling me. They have the blessing of the ancient yews, those born in the Forestwife's clearing, and I have to agree that your Robert is a very remarkable fellow. Something or someone has certainly blessed him!'

As they entered the hut they breathed in the woody scent of fresh marjoram. A sense of calm filled the small room; Robert seemed to be resting quietly, propped up on the straw pallet. He looked a lot cleaner, his cheeks flushed slightly pink.

Marian crouched down at his side and put her hand on his forehead. 'Much better,' she sighed with relief. 'So much better. What have you done?'

Brigit and Gerta sat by the fire, smiling and pleased with themselves. 'It's the little lass,' Gerta insisted. 'I helped and I did as she told me, but it was the lass's idea, not mine. We dragged him round to the spring and bathed him – dunked him right in the water. It seemed to soothe him, so we let him have a right good soaking. Then we hauled him out and rubbed him down well with dried lavender and soft lamb's wool.'

'It seems you've done right.' Philippa laughed. 'He looks better than he has since that rock smashed down on his head.'

Marian sniffed at the drained wooden mug that stood on the rushes. 'Marjoram tea?' she asked.

Brigit nodded. 'Mother always said it was good for the head and it was you that told me that the warm spring was magical!'

'I don't know that I'd have had the courage to just dunk him in,' said Marian. 'Your mother taught you well, Brigit. You are turning into a fine little herbwife.'

Robert slept soundly, all through the afternoon and the next night. He woke the following morning still weak, but recognising them. Marian made him rest and fed him well, full of joy and confidence in his recovery. Though she'd feared him lost beyond hope, her man had returned to her yet again.

As the last days of July came, the charcoal burners and coal-diggers set aside their spades and stacks and gathered at Langden, ready to help with the harvest work. Lammas-tide celebrated the start of the cutting of the wheat, oats and barley.

Magda loved this time of year, for the first job to be done was not the cutting of the crops, but the clearing out of all the stale stinking rushes that covered the floor of each cottage and hut. The gathering and bringing home of fresh rushes brought the sweet smells of wood-land and strewing herbs into every dwelling.

'We must have a feast now,' she told Marian. 'Asking for blessings on the harvest is important. You have always said so.'

'You and your feasts,' Marian laughed. But then a shadow of anxiety seemed to touch her face. 'But, yes,' she said solemnly. 'You are right! We must ask blessings on our harvest, before we cut and then be sure to give thanks afterwards. The harvest is always precious, but this year it shall be most precious indeed. And the gleaning. The gleaning must be done so carefully. Not an ear of corn, not a flake of oat must be left behind.'

Magda was pleased to have her feast and she did not notice the anxiety that lay hidden behind Marian's words. Lammastide brought a fine moonlit night and the clearing was filled with the smells of fresh rushes and roast venison, and they sang and danced until it was late.

Though the harvest made everyone work desperately hard, still a great joyfulness seemed to fill the clearing. So often the women had worked alone, but this year was different. Marian had expected Robert to proclaim himself fit, and go marching off to join some rebel baron, but this time even he spoke of staying to help with the work. If Robert was happy to stay, then so were Tom and James and many more.

As Robert's strength returned he even busied himself about the clearing, cutting firewood, reeds and rushes, and mending the leaking thatch. He left the wild safety of Barnsdale Woods only to make the occasional foray into Sherwood, returning with welcome fresh meat, venison or sometimes wild boar. The only ones who seemed unsettled were John and James. They spent much time together deep in conversation, and John, who had always loved the company of his friends, often wandered off without saying a word or telling anyone where he was going.

Marian had never been so happy. Since his bang on the head Robert seemed more gentle and loving than ever before. 'I swear that flying stone did me a favour,' she teased as they sat on the doorsill in the late afternoon sun. 'I could have done with it giving you a good thump on the head twenty years ago.'

Robert chuckled. 'Put down those stinking herbs and come here, sweetheart,' he begged.

Marian hesitated. 'There is much to do,' she told him.

'Aye,' he agreed. 'But who knows what tomorrow may bring us? This scarred old wolf thinks himself very lucky to have fought so many battles and still be here with his mate, sitting in the sun.'

Marian sighed, but she stopped her work and went to him. Tom and Magda returned with James from Isabel's fields at dusk and found them fast asleep, propping each other up, while herbs blew about in the dust and chickens pecked at their feet.

The Forestwife's cottage became very cramped with so many people and through many a warm night they ended up sleeping outside beneath the stars. Then one evening as they sat by the fire, exhausted and aching, Tom put his arm around Magda and told them that he had something to say.

Marian looked up in surprise, for Magda was usually

the one that did any telling there was to be done. The younger woman had been somewhat quiet of late, though she and Tom seemed closer than they had ever been.

'We are going to build another hut, Magda and I,' said Tom. 'There are too many of us to cramp together in Marian's cottage when the cool of autumn comes.'

Marian raised her eyebrows and smiled. So, they planned to stay through the winter months too, did they?

'Aye,' John agreed. 'You're right, but where will you build it?'

'Close by,' Magda told him, though she glanced worriedly at Marian.

'Then we'll all help,' Robert said cheerfully. 'As soon as the harvesting is done, we'll set to work. It must be done before the weather turns. 'Tis better by far to spend our time building homes than fighting battles we can never win.'

John and James looked up at each other surprised but not displeased.

'Aye,' said James. 'My old bones would enjoy spending a winter by a warm fire for once.'

Marian was pleased at the plans but, as she looked at Magda's troubled face, a suspicion came to her. Brigit said nothing, but listened to it all a touch anxiously.

The following morning Magda moved to join the harvesting team, but Marian called her back. 'Robert goes with them,' she said. 'You stay here with me today. I think there is something else to be told. Don't forget, I know you very well my girl.' She set about scouring her cooking pots with a handful of sand. 'Come, sit down here beside me while I work,' she said. 'Now . . . tell me.'

Magda looked miserable, but did as she was told. 'You'll be angry,' she said.

'Huh!' Marian laughed. 'Since when have you feared my anger?'

Magda smiled, but her brow still creased with concern. 'I did not do what you taught me,' she said quietly. 'You told me many ways to stop a bairn from starting to grow, but I did not use them.'

'As I thought,' Marian nodded.

'More than that,' Magda gasped. 'I went out on Brig's night and made a bower and a Biddy doll. I begged for a bairn and Brig has sent me one. I thought it was Brigit that she'd sent at first, but now I have my own bairn coming too.'

Marian stared at her, surprised. 'You should have told me.'

'There is still more.' Now that she had started telling, it all came tumbling out in a rush. 'I want to marry Tom and be his wife. I want everyone to wish us joy and to know that he is my man, but you told me that the Forest-wife should never marry. You always refused Robert, whenever he wished to be wed to you.'

'Aye,' said Marian. 'That is what I told you, isn't it?'

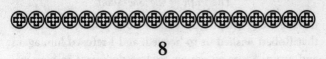

8

Under the Trysting Tree

They were both silent then, and all that could be heard was the crackle of the fire and the harsh scouring sound as Marian worked grains of sand around the pot.

'You chose never to have a child,' Magda whispered at last. 'You told me that being Forestwife was too important . . . and that I should be Forestwife after you. But I do not think that I am the right one. Little Brigit would make a better Forestwife; she has more knowledge of herbs and potions than I will ever have. She does not even need to be taught, she just knows. I think now that Brig sent her here to take my place.'

Marian stopped her scouring and dropped the bowl; she moved to Magda and put her arms around her. 'You must have wanted this bairn very much,' she said.

Magda nodded and buried her face in Marian's shoulder. They rocked together gently, both of them turning tearful.

'All will be well, all will be well,' Marian soothed. Then she heaved a great sigh. 'Of late I seem to look back on my life and wonder why I made such decisions. It's true that Robert wished us to be wed, and I refused him again and again. I was so young, and so desperate to play my part, wishing to right all wrongs. I charged into every battle that came our way, fighting for those who could not fight.'

'And you have done it,' Magda told her. 'You have saved many and made life bearable for those who would have suffered terribly. Every struggling peasant in Barnsdale has faith in the Forestwife and the Hooded One.'

'Aye,' Marian nodded. 'And I believed that I could not do it and be tied to a man. Now I come to think that I was too hard on myself, and also on those around me. I regret it much of late. I have learned that no matter how hard you fight, however much you sacrifice, still you can never win.'

'No,' Magda agreed smiling. 'But it is still better to fight.'

'Yes. You have learned that, so much younger than I did. It is just . . . keeping up the struggle that really matters, and there is one more thing that's important for you to know. I have never wanted to bear a child for I had you to mother. I never wanted another child but you.'

Magda smiled at that and kissed her, then doubt crossed her face again. 'The Forestwife? The sacred trust?'

Marian shook her head. 'You shall be Forestwife, I am sure of it, but maybe Brig did send Brigit to us. Perhaps you need not do the work alone. Brigit is a wonderful healer, that's true, but there is more to being Forestwife than that. How many times have I put aside my potions and taken up my bow and gone running through the woods ready to fight? Can Brigit do that? I know that you can!'

Magda nodded. 'It's true, the work is not all healing wounds; you have done some fierce and terrible things.'

'And you have always been there at my side, spurring me on, giving me courage. That is the work of the Forest-wife just as much as tending the sick. I grow a little tired these days; and come to think that we three might share the work; Brigit the maiden, you the mother, and I the Old One.'

'You are not the Old One yet!' Magda insisted, and Marian was glad to see the happiness back in her eyes.

'No, 'Marian agreed. 'And if you wish to marry your Tom, go and do so. Go and tell Tom that you will marry him.'

Magda laughed. 'I haven't even spoken of it to him yet!'

Tom was willing enough, and as the harvest work went on they planned to have a late August wedding beneath the trysting tree. They'd celebrate the young couple's wedding, along with the cutting of the last sheaf of corn.

Every harvest was the same; Isabel always brought the last sheaf from Langden through the woods to the Forest-wife's clearing. They'd twist and plait the stook until it took on the shape of a woman that they called the Corn Goddess; then they'd crown it with a wreath of flowers, and feast and dance around it, giving thanks and praise for the harvest brought safely in.

When the last few days of corn cutting came Marian

insisted on going to Langden to make sure the gleaning was done thoroughly, but the rest of her friends stayed in the clearing and started work on Magda's new home. The woods rang with the sounds of hammering and the crack of splitting wood. Orders were shouted by Magda and ignored by most as their hands, already toughened with harvest work, grew strong as leather. They wove wattle panels that they stuffed with goats' hair and chicken feathers, then coated them with mud and left them to dry in the sun. With everyone helping the work was swiftly done.

Once the panels were dried out in the late August sun, they fixed them onto a small but sturdy timber frame and set a hearth stone in the middle. They thatched the roof beams, leaving a small hole for smoke to come through. Magda was filled with excitement as the first wisps of smoke rose upward from the fire that she'd lit, drifting out through the hole 'Where is Tom, where is Brigit?' she cried. 'Fetch the rugs and bedding in!'

Brigit who'd helped quietly throughout the building work looked stunned. She stood there open mouthed. 'Am I . . .?'

'Why yes,' Magda cried, hugging her tightly. 'Did I not make it clear? You are to come and live here with us and be my family.'

'Oh,' Brigit's face glowed. 'I didn't know. I thought you'd like to be alone with Tom.'

'Believe me,' said Magda, hands on hips. 'When Tom goes off adventuring with Robert in the spring, as I know he will, and I have a tiny babe to rear, then I am going to need you very much.'

So Magda ruled her new home with bossy pleasure, while John and James settled themselves in the lean-to with Fetcher to keep them warm, and Robert and Marian were left alone and happy in the cottage like any old husband and wife.

The day of Magda's wedding dawned bright and sunny. 'See,' Marian pointed out. 'Brig is smiling on you still.'

Isabel arrived from Langden with the last cut sheaf and Philippa in the back of her wagon. Will Stoutley drove them, and they were all dressed in fine new clothes of scarlet cloth, and somehow looking very pleased with themselves.

Marian dressed in her only gown, a patched and worn green kirtle, suddenly felt very old and tired. 'You look as though you are thriving, all of you,' she told them.

'Oh we are thriving as never before, especially some of us,' Philippa said, laughing and nodding towards Isabel and Will. 'This has been a fine harvest,' she told Marian. 'We've little to fear this winter.'

Marian pressed her lips together, biting back words of doubt, but then she smiled. 'I pray that's true,' she said.

The Sisters of the Magdalen arrived with little posies fastened to their veils, excited and chattering, for Magda wished them to take part in her celebrations. Then a great gang of ragged children from the woodland cottages came skipping and dancing into the clearing, carrying more small posies. They surrounded Magda's new home, chanting:

> *'Here we bring our posies,*
> *Our garlands, and our roses.*
> *Bring her out! Bring her out!*
> *So we can greet the harvest bride.'*

Then to cheers and clapping the newly woven door curtain was thrown aside and out came Magda and Tom, both wearing new green dyed kirtles and crowned with flowers.

John took up his pipe, James beat a deerskin drum, while Fetcher pranced about his master and a happy procession formed behind the young couple. They led the dance around the clearing, pausing for a while beside the beautiful, bubbling warm spring that gave so much aid and comfort to Marian's most sickly visitors.

The children danced around the spring, singing:

> *'Blessings on the water,*
> *Blessings on the sea,*
> *Blessings on the woodland streams,*
> *And blessings on me.'*

Then they threw their small posies into its clear waters where they bobbed up and down.

Suddenly the procession was moving on and round to the trysting tree. The Sisters of the Magdalen waited there, standing in a half-circle around the last cut sheaf of corn

that Isabel and Philippa had plaited and twisted cleverly
into the shape of the goddess. It stood in the middle of
them, shoulder high and crowned with a beautiful wreath
of ears of corn and flowers.

Magda and Tom exchanged their vows beneath the
trysting tree, and the nuns and brother James spoke their
blessings. Then, as they kissed, everyone clapped and
cheered. Magda turned to lead the dance back past the
goddess towards the cottage, where a long trestle table
stood, bearing bread, fruit, cheese and ale, but much to
everyone's surprise Philippa strode out from the watching
crowd and announced that another happy event was to
take place.

'Come on,' she ordered, and Isabel came forward
blushing and smiling, Will Stoutley at her side.

'I thought never to marry,' Isabel announced. 'As you
all know, I fought bitterly against it, and many of you paid
a heavy price for my freedom. Now, at last I have found a
man that I can trust, and truly love. Will Stoutley is
the man I freely choose to be my husband, and I beg you
all bear witness to our vows?'

'Aye! Aye!' everyone bellowed with approval.

So there and then, both dressed in fine new scarlet,
Isabel married Will beneath the trysting tree.

'Now to dance around the goddess,' Magda cried.

'No . . . not yet,' another voice rang out.

Everyone turned and this time it was Robert who came
forward, and he held up his hand for quiet. A sudden
hush fell. When Robert decided to speak, there was no
knowing what was coming next; a sudden joy, or a snat-

ching up of weapons and a mad scheme that would leave the woodland half empty, and women and children alone and struggling.

But this time Robert had a wicked and cheerful gleam in his eye. He prowled around the Corn Goddess, and nobody moved or spoke; even the children were quiet. He stopped before Marian. 'There is so much joy and happiness here today,' he said. 'That I too dare once more to beg a favour that I have had refused so many times before. Marian, I beg you . . . marry me now, at last, here in this loving circle of friends.'

Everyone turned quiet again, shocked and surprised, straining to hear the reply. This was a joyful day, but the Forestwife belonged to the people of the woods, and not to any man. For a moment Marian looked lost and unsure, but then she pressed her lips tightly together, shaking her head.

'Nay,' she told him firmly. 'Though I love you better than life itself, we have chosen a different way – you and I. There will be no wedding for the Forestwife and the Hooded One.'

Robert flinched staring down at the straw-strewn earth beneath their feet, his thin scarred face grim. His friends watched in silence, dreading his anger, seeing his humiliation. But they needn't have feared for suddenly he smiled broadly, and swung back to being his usual teasing self. 'Maybe you are right, my Green Lady – perhaps I'd have been shocked if you'd agreed. Will you still dance with me?'

'I will always dance with you,' she whispered. 'But I am no Green Lady – not anymore.'

Robert turned and snatched up the beautiful flower-woven garland from the Corn Goddess, and placed it on Marian's head. 'No. You've become the Corn Goddess,' he cried. 'Beautiful and golden, touched with sorrow and sun. Now dance with me!'

'Yes,' she whispered.

'Now can we all dance?' Magda cried at last.

Though the feast was small, everyone was joyful at the day's events, and the singing and dancing went on till dawn.

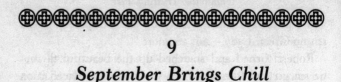

9

September Brings Chill

After the excitement of the woodland weddings it was hard to settle down and return to the autumn work that must be done. But as the weather turned cooler Marian returned to her usual practical preparations for the winter ahead. Nobody was allowed to sit and dream, and each day they went out into the woods returning with baskets and sacks full of mushrooms, berries, nuts and herbs.

Magda was so busy with her new home that she did not at first notice the strange restlessness that seemed to surround her father. John would wake early in the mornings and be off without telling anyone where he was going, then appear again late at night, quiet and tired with a bag half filled with firewood or a handful of yew staves. The only one he really spoke to was James. Despite her distraction even Magda noticed at last. She was puzzled. Robert was usually the unsettled one and John the calmer, more contented of the two men.

'Father's gone off again this morning,' she told Tom. 'Gone off without saying a word. I don't know what it is with him! Half the time I feel as though his mind is somewhere else.'

Tom did not look as surprised as she'd expected, but he sighed and then began to speak gently. 'Aye, I think his mind is often somewhere else, and I believe I know what it is that disturbs the man's peace.'

'Then tell me!' Magda demanded.

'Well,' said Tom. 'It all started when we marched down to Northampton to join the Bishop. We fell in with a gang of men sent down from Derbyshire. They were sent down to fight for their rebel lord, the constable of Peveril Castle, in the land they call The Peak.'

'Aye, and so?' Magda was impatient.

'Well, there was a fellow who knew John, the moment he clapped eyes on him. He came from the village of Hathersage.'

'Ah!' Magda began to understand. 'Hathersage where my father was born and raised?'

Tom nodded. 'The two of them marched side by side for days and whispered by the fire all night. They'd watched over sheep on the hillsides together when they were lads and believe me I have never known John to take such delight in talking as he did with that fellow.'

Magda frowned, unsure that she liked the sound of it. She herself had never known this distant Derbyshire village. She'd been born in the Forestwife's clearing, and that had been the centre of all her life.

'What did they talk about?' she asked.

'People, places, names they both knew. Wild adventures of their youth! The old ones who'd died, and some young ones too.' Tom sighed. 'It brought John great pleasure,' he said. 'But I think it brought him sadness too.'

'And so this man, this old friend of my father's returned to Hathersage?'

Tom shook his head. 'That is the greatest sadness of it all. He was caught like Robert by one of the great stone-throwing machines. He was not as lucky as Robert was, for he died. So you see, there was no returning to Hathersage, not for him. Now,' Tom asked gently. 'Do you understand John's restlessness a bit better?'

Magda heaved a great sigh. 'Oh yes,' she said. 'I understand it very well, though I do not much like the answer that comes into my mind.'

'No,' Tom shook his head sadly. 'No, I thought you would not. That is why I never spoke of it before.'

Magda smiled at him, and patted her stomach that was beginning to swell quite noticeably. 'Ah well,' she said determinedly. 'I have got my wish. Father shall have his wish too, whether he thinks he should or not. Would you travel with him to see him safely there?'

Tom smiled at her. 'Of course I will.'

She went out into the woods, following the path her father had taken. Two days later, John set out for Hathersage, riding behind Tom on Rambler's strong back. John was reluctant to leave his daughter, but the quiet joy in his eyes at the thought of returning to his childhood home was there for all to see.

'You go with my blessing,' Magda told him, sounding stronger than she felt. 'All I ask is that you come back to us at Christmas, for my child should be born soon after that.'

No sooner had John and Tom set out for Derbyshire than Philippa's blacksmith husband returned to Langden with Rowan her son. Philippa walked through the woodland paths to pass their news on to the Forestwife and her friends. She gently touched Brigit's head as she passed the child, sitting out in the autumn sunshine, steadily pounding dandelion roots.

'Are they inside?' she asked.

'Yes,' Brigit sighed. 'They do nothing but talk of the barons and the King.'

Philippa went inside and joined them by the fireside. She told of her husband's return. 'I feared he'd never get paid for all his work, and if the barons had had their way, he never would.'

'Who has paid him?' Robert asked.

Philippa smiled. 'Your friend, the Bishop of Hereford.'

Robert looked up, interested. 'I knew that man was different. The other bishops went running to side with the King as soon as they heard the pope had denounced the charter. Not Giles de Braose, even though we distrust them, the Bishop of Hereford still stands by the rebel barons.'

'Ah well,' Philippa cleared her throat. 'I'm not so sure. The King has tried to buy the man's loyalty back again. He's offered him the de Braose property fully restored, and all his dead brother's land, but the Bishop must swear fealty once more.'

'And what does the man reply?' Robert leant forward.

Philippa shrugged her shoulders. 'We don't know yet, and I have sadder news,' she sighed. 'News that will bring great sorrow to that little lass out there, who pounds roots as though her life depends on it.'

'Oh no,' Magda cried. 'Not Brigit's father!'

Philippa nodded. 'The man is dead. The King sent his wolfpack to take back the Tower of London. The barons had given way and agreed that it should be held in the Archbishop of Canterbury's name, but some of those who'd been defending it resisted. Brigit's father was one of them.'

Magda got up, her face all creased with pity. 'I'll tell her,' she said. 'I don't want to, but I will.'

Brigit took the news of her father's death quietly, but during the next few days she wandered aimlessly about the clearing as though she'd lost all purpose in life. Marian praised her herb skills and begged her help with the potions and simples, but the young girl refused politely. Magda followed her at a distance, feeling useless and somehow responsible. 'I wished for a bairn, Brig,' she murmured. 'And you sent Brigit that very night. Now she has nobody else but me.'

Concern for Brigit's sadness reached as far as Langden and one afternoon towards the end of September, Isabel arrived from Langden driving a small grain cart, with Philippa seated in the back.

Marian went to greet them, smiling; this visit was not entirely unexpected. Brigit looked up listlessly from the new doorsill. Magda marched over and mercilessly hauled the young girl to her feet. 'You have to come and see what Isabel has brought,' she ordered.

'Why?' Brigit cried, surprised and hurt by her friend's rough treatment.

'Come and see,' Magda insisted, pulling her round to the back of the cart.

'But I . . . oh!' Brigit's mouth dropped open in surprise. For there in Philippa's lap rolled a plump, well-fed, baby boy, dressed in a soft lamb's wool smock. His thatch of curly hair was the same golden brown as Brigit's, his cheeks pink as a wild rose.

'Is . . . is he?'

'Yes,' Isabel told her. 'He is your brother Peterkin, that you named for your father. His foster mother has fed and cared for him well, but now he's weaned from the breast and drinking goats' milk. He's a lively lad and his foster mother has her own children to see to.'

'Do you mean? Should I . . .?'

'We thought that Peterkin might like to be with his sister,' said Isabel.

'But . . .' said Brigit, hesitating. 'But, I am very busy here. I don't know whether I can look after him, and still fetch the wood and pick the herbs and crush the roots.'

The women laughed and Magda put her arms around Brigit. 'If you want him here, then I should like to help look after him. We might share the job but only if you want that.'

Brigit took a step towards the cart and the wriggling baby. Philippa scooped him up and handed him to his sister. The girl put his chin gently to rest against her

73

shoulder. She sniffed his soft hair and rubbed her cheek against it. Warm dribble tickled her neck, making her giggle. 'Oh yes,' she said, patting him gently on the back. 'Yes. Please let Peterkin stay.'

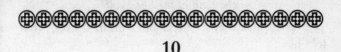

Through October and November the weather turned damp and chilly. Everyone wrapped up well and worked on, building up their stocks of nuts and meat for the very cold weather still to come. Sherwood and the surrounding wastes and woodlands were full of pigs, allowed to wander and forage freely for a short period of time in the pannage month so that they could gorge themselves on acorns and beech mast, fattening themselves up for the coming harsh months. Tom returned from Hathersage with news of the warm welcome that John had received.

'He is famous there!' Tom told them. 'They all know John of Hathersage who walks with the Hooded One. They treat him like a king and regale him with the stories of his doings. Some are true, but half of them are rubbish. John laughs and puts them straight but still they tell the tales. I shall go back to Derbyshire and fetch him home for you in time for Christmas,' he promised Magda.

'Will he be safe there?' Robert asked with unusual concern.

75

'I believe that they'd defend him with their lives,' Tom told him.

Now that Tom was back, more hunting trips were made to Sherwood and Marian salted and smoked the meat that they brought. The woodlanders always gathered and picked feverishly at this time of year, for the result meant the difference between eating or starving, life or death, but this year Marian worked more tirelessly than ever.

'Even acorns,' she insisted. 'What's good for pigs is good for us! However bitter they may taste, ground-up acorns can keep body and soul together, and we must fetch nettles to dry and crumble and blackthorn berries and juniper too.'

'Haven't we got enough?' Magda complained. 'You'll wear yourself away to nothing if you don't stop. You'll have us gathering up the dust beneath our feet and storing it away for the snows.'

Marian hesitated, her brow creased. 'It's just that I have a terrible sense of urgency come upon me. Almost like . . . like my mother, Eleanor. You remember how she knew when things were going to go wrong.'

'Aye?' Magda was suddenly attentive.

'And somehow I know that we must gather and gather, and not let one precious grain go to waste. I have other fears too; last week I thought I saw Robert's mother, Agnes, down by the spring washing clothes.'

'You saw her spirit?' Magda gasped.

'I believe I did, but it wasn't fearful. I could never fear Agnes for she loved me well, but as she scrubbed and washed I thought the water swam with blood. Then I blinked and she had vanished.'

Magda shivered and pressed her hands to her swelling stomach. 'Your mother did have the sight,' she agreed seriously 'And she always saw true.'

Marian quickly understood the younger woman's anxiety and went to place her own hand on Magda's stomach. ''Tis not for this growing child that I see trouble. I think Agnes was giving warning for myself or maybe Robert.'

'Aye,' Magda spoke with some relief. 'Robert would be the one.'

'Yes,' said Marian. 'But do not speak of it to him, and certainly do not fear for this little one; I see nothing but happiness there.'

Magda was soothed a little. 'Don't you worry about Robert either,' she said. 'He's safer here than anywhere and he doesn't seem at all inclined to go off to join either Robert de Ros or another northern Lord.'

'Aye,' Marian agreed. 'As they grow older they seem less ready for the fight, and I for one am very glad of it.'

'My Tom's not old,' Magda insisted.

'No he is not,' Marian agreed. 'But then your Tom has never been one for rushing into the attack; he has more sense. But still, he's no coward; when there's something desperately needs doing, he's the one that's always there, quietly risking himself.'

'I know it,' Magda murmured.

'It's strange,' Marian sighed. 'I do not want Robert to go away adventuring,' she whispered, her eyes suddenly swimming with tears, 'but I cannot see him staying close by my side forever. How can I keep a wild wolf-man such as he, tamed like a tabby cat to sit by my fireside?'

Various, well-armed expeditions were made by the sheriff and his men to the outskirts of the woods. These fruitless searches gave much amusement to those who lived outside the law and wild new rumours spread.

'Can you believe it?' Gerta told Marian and Philippa as they sifted through the crackling leaves beneath a chestnut tree. 'It's whispered that the Sheriff has this strange idea that the Hooded One might be a woman!'

Gerta continued digging her foot into the ground to drag aside the mushy green skins, leaving shining brown nuts exposed.

'No!' Marian looked up smiling, her hands full of the prickly fruit.

'Oh yes! Any woman caught running wild through the woods is to be searched for weapons! Though it seems his soldiers do not often venture very far into the woods, for they fear the Forestwife's curse on them!'

Marian clapped her hand to her mouth, choking with laughter.

Philippa hugged her, snorting at the joke. 'I can't think why the Sheriff could think such a thing! What could poor women such as us do? Pelt his men with sweet chestnuts?'

'No!' Marian howled, slapping Philippa's large backside. 'Now why should the silly man think that the Hooded One could be a woman?'

Gerta smiled, understanding their mirth, but still her

expression was troubled. 'Even nuns are to be stopped and searched,' she said. 'For the Sheriff declares that no respectable nun should be out walking through the woods either alone or with her sisters.'

Marian turned solemn when she heard that and she looked at Philippa with concern. 'Have we put the Sisters of the Magdalen in danger?'

The taller woman shrugged her shoulders. 'We did what we thought best. We have always done that.'

Marian's fears that Robert might turn into a tabby cat were soon put to flight for one morning in mid November Brother James and Philippa came riding fast through the woods from Langden with frightening news.

'You must get up off your backside,' the plump monk told his friend as he burst into the cottage, his face all red and shaking. 'They've got Will and taken him off to Clipston. The Sheriff is there and arranging a hanging!'

Robert was on his feet in a moment. 'How have they got Will? And why hang him?'

'Did they ever need a good reason? A gang of the Sheriff's men turned up at Langden. Isabel got a little warning for some of the coal-diggers saw the gang of mercenaries heading towards the manor.'

'Why Langden?' Marian asked.

'It seems the Lady of Langden has been recognised and reported as one of the women who helped to rescue Gerta's grandsons.'

'I feared something like that!' Marian said quietly.

'Will insisted that Isabel took to the woods,' Philippa

told them hurriedly. 'But then he stayed to see all the servants safely away and out of the hall. He did not manage to escape in time himself.'

'What do they want with Will?' Robert asked.

'I fear they may think they've got you,' Brother James cried. 'They bellowed and shouted that they'd got the Hooded One, and Will killed two of their men, before they could get hold of him.'

'Aye,' Philippa added. 'It's either that, or the Sheriff tries his hand at a different, more crafty way of getting at thee! But we must not stand here asking why! We must do something and fast. Tom has gone riding off after them on Rambler, but what can Tom do on his own? Rowan and Isabel are gathering together the servants, but they are just a tiny handful and they are farmers, none of them are fighting men!'

'Damnation,' Robert growled. 'Where can we get help from quickly? All those who fought with us for the charter have returned to their homes. It would take days to get them together.'

'I know,' cried Magda. 'The answer's there right in front of our noses. The woods are crowded out with pig-herders. The pannage finishes tomorrow, but they're still there today, getting every last scrap they can for their beasts.'

Robert stared at her, puzzled. 'But they are children and old folk!'

Marian quickly picked up the way that Magda was thinking. 'Yes,' she said. 'But there are so many of them. If we start marching towards Clipston, and beg the pig-herders to join us, we shall pass hundreds of them.'

Robert hesitated. 'But . . . will they be willing?'

'Yes,' Marian spoke with confidence. 'They'll be very angry and willing once they know that it is Isabel's new husband that is at risk! How many of them received gifts of grain from Langden in the harshest days last winter? How many of them wear a warm cloak, woven with wool from Isabel's sheep? The news of Isabel's marriage has spread far and wide and brought much happiness with it!'

Suddenly Robert laughed, and kissed Magda on the nose. 'You are a clever lass! It is mad, but it just might save the man!'

So though he felt a little unsure that they'd got the strength for this fight, Robert threw himself into action, gathering together all the bows and weapons that they could. They left the clearing soon after noon. Marian marched with them, insisting that Magda stay behind with Gerta and Brigit, the Forestwife's girdle fastened carefully around her stomach.

Peasant, Fool or Rebel Lord

Though Clipston was small compared to the great castle of Nottingham, the walls were solid and sturdy, built of strong, sandy-coloured local stone. The place was a hunting lodge, built to house the King comfortably when he chose to go chasing the fine Sherwood deer.

Sheriff de Rue went out to meet the gang of returning soldiers. They were delighted with the prisoner that they'd found, though still uncertain exactly who he was. Will rode amongst them in silence, with his head held high, even though they'd bound his arms behind his back and fastened his legs to the saddle.

'Who is this?' the Sheriff demanded. 'Haven't you got the woman?'

The men shook their heads and shuffled their feet. 'No sign of her,' they said. 'Just this fellow, defending the place alone. We think we've maybe got the Hooded One for you.'

'What makes you think that?'

'The fellow killed two of our men before we managed to get him.'

The Sheriff looked at Will with uncertainty. 'Who are you?' he asked quietly.

Will smiled proudly, ''Tis as they say,' he agreed. 'I be the Hooded One.'

The Sheriff was puzzled. The man bore himself with great dignity and wore a fine scarlet mantle but spoke like a peasant. 'Who the devil is this Hooded One?' he muttered to himself. 'Is he peasant, fool, or rebel lord?'

'Put him in the lock-up,' at last he snarled. 'Whoever he is, he'll hang before the sun goes down.'

Will did not flinch or tremble as they led him away.

A gibbet was fast erected outside the walls of Clipston and a short while before the sun began to set, the great wooden gates opened and Will Stoutley was escorted outside, his hands still tied. The Sheriff came down from the ornate stateroom that he used himself while the king was not in residence. De Rue was still uncertain exactly who this prisoner was; but the man had killed two guards and that were a grievous enough offence to hang him without hesitation.

As Will was led out towards the gibbet, a fair-haired man emerged from the sheltering trees, and dismounted quietly from his horse. He moved slowly towards the raised platform, limping slightly and gripping the handle of a dagger that was stuck into his belt. His other hand, apparently, rested carelessly on the hilt of his sword.

The scarlet-coated figure of Will strode up the new-made steps. He glanced at the small crowd of foresters and soldiers and saw the face of a friend down there below him. No sign of recognition crossed his face; instead he turned to speak to the Sheriff. 'Let me die an honourable death,' he cried. 'Let me die as befits the Hooded One with a sword in my hand.'

A sneer touched the Sheriff's thin lips. He laughed: then spat into Will's face. 'Hang the fool,' he cried. 'Get on with it! Shut his stupid mouth up! Shut it forever!'

As the hangman moved to lift the noose, suddenly Tom was swinging himself up onto the platform with agility, despite his damaged leg, sword and dagger in his hands. He sliced through Will's bonds in a moment.

Will laughed, delighted.

'Here's your sword,' Tom cried. 'Don't die with honour; fight instead! Help shall come – I'm sure of it!'

Then the two men swung about back to back as they'd so often done in their practising. Will with a sword and Tom with his dagger were both ready to fight to the death any and all of the Sheriff's men.

The Sheriff howled with anger. 'Kill them! Kill them both!' he screamed.

But the guards hesitated to charge at them, for the gleam that was there in the outlaws' eyes told them that they would not die without taking others with them.

Then all at once an arrow went whistling over the heads of the soldiers, just grazing the Sheriff's cheek. The Sheriff swung round in fury as more arrows flew out from the edge of the woodland bringing down two more soldiers.

Then there started up strange distant thudding sounds that grew and grew, at last becoming thunderously loud.

'Look out! Look out!' one of the soldiers cried, pointing towards the woods. Everybody turned to see that the bushes and branches on the edge of the forest were trembling and shaking. Even tall trees twisted and turned, waving wildly about. All at once hundreds of squealing, grunting pigs came bursting out from the shadows of the trees, charging at speed towards the platform and the crowd of fighting men. There was sudden wild panic, every man shouting at his companions, nobody able to hear or make sense.

'Ya! Ya!' came the cries of the herders as they still drove the pigs on. The gibbet was surrounded by fat, heaving, snorting bodies. More arrows whistled overhead and the Sheriff was grazed again in the elbow. He did not wait to see what next might come flying out from the forest, but fought his way through the charging beasts, slicing his sword in all directions, heading for the gates of Clipston. At last he reached the safety of the courtyard, his men streaming after him.

'Get back and fight them,' he cried, 'I order you back!'

The Sheriff tried to close the gates and make his men stay and fight, but they'd had enough of nasty surprises for one day and only when the last guard was eventually safe inside did they swing the gates closed.

There was just a moment of laughter and rejoicing, then the outlaws took action once again knowing that they must not hang about. Isabel rode straight at the collapsing gibbet and hauled Will up behind her onto her strong grey mare. Tom whistled for Rambler and in a moment the horse was by his side. There were a few more shouts and sharp bursts of laughter as the pigs were quickly rounded up and driven back into the woods. When the Sheriff dared to open the gates once more there was nothing left but a smashed gibbet and a great expanse of trampled ground and pig-muck.

'Get into the woods,' the Sheriff cried. 'Kill every pig-herder you can find. Kill every pig!'

But as the night grew darker, the pigs and their owners left the woodlands, slipping away to their homes along the secret paths that they knew well. A thin mist rose from the sodden mossy grass, growing thicker in patches, sending the soldiers stumbling about, lost and weary. They fell into bogs and streams, cursing the pigs and their herders, cursing each other but cursing the Sheriff most of all.

There was much joy as Will and his rescuers returned to Langden, but Marian marched ahead of the others towards the Forestwife's clearing, her face grim.

'Do not look so anxious,' Robert begged, running after her. 'It was a mad idea, that you and Magda thought up, but it worked!'

'Aye. It worked,' she agreed. 'But the Sheriff will not forget Langden now! This will not be the end of it. We have made a fool of him, but this man's no buffoon like the last Sheriff was! He will not forgive or forget this night's work.'

Robert frowned and nodded but still his smile returned and he took hold of her hand. 'You are right as ever, but I tell you this. I would not have missed the look on de Rue's face when all the pigs charged out from the trees . . . I would not have missed it for the world! And I do not think this Sheriff will return to Langden in a hurry!'

'No, maybe not,' Marian relented and smiled at last. She moved closer to Robert and they marched along together, arms about each other's waists, their pace matching perfectly, step for step.

Though the soldiers spent a few more days scouring Sherwood for pigs and herders, there were none to be found. The pannage month was over and they'd all gone back to their villages. Robert once more took up his quiet fireside job of whittling arrow shafts and gathering goose feathers to make the flights.

12
King John's Revenge

In early December Tom set off for Hathersage, while Isabel and Philippa brought news that they'd picked up from travellers passing through Langden. King John had destroyed Rochester Castle by tunnelling beneath the ground and blowing up one of the towers with a huge explosion of fire and pig fat. He'd then marched on to Winchester and was said to be gathering together more arms and even more mercenaries.

'He's setting out from St Albans now, heading for Northampton,' Isabel told them.

Robert exchanged uneasy glances with James. 'I don't like the sound of him marching north. The farther he is from us the better,' he muttered.

'There's sad news of the rebellious Bishop of Hereford,' Isabel added. 'He agreed at last to swear fealty again, but the deed was never done. The man has died.'

'Indeed?' Robert growled. 'Then he never forgave the King. I cannot say I'm sorry! Let's hope this brings an end to that family's suffering.'

Everyone murmured agreement to that.

'There's a stranger story going about,' said Isabel. 'I can't believe it's true, but they say that the rebel barons have sent envoys to the King of France, begging him to send his son Prince Louis at the head of an army.'

'Why should the French come to England's aid?' Robert asked.

'They promise that if he support the rebel barons in their fight and help them get rid of King John, then in return they shall make Prince Louis our king.'

There were gasps from them all.

'What? It doesn't make sense,' Robert insisted. 'What good would it do to have another foreign king brought here? What does Prince Louis know of us?'

'Huh! It doesn't surprise me,' Marian told them. 'The barons simply seek another way to snatch power for themselves.'

'You best tell them about Robert de Ros,' Philippa prompted.

'Yes,' Isabel agreed. 'The great northerner lord returned to his castle at Helmsley, as soon as he heard that the King's army travels north. He's setting about building up his defences as though he expects a siege.'

'Aye,' Philippa added. 'And he is not the only baron who does that. They all seem to expect the worst and where does it leave us?'

'Defenceless! And right in the middle of it all, as usual!' Marian spoke with anger.

'We are not defenceless,' Magda cried. 'We must do what we've always done. We'll fight!'

'Aye Magda,' Philippa smiled. 'But you will not be doing the fighting this time. You'll leave that to us.'

Marian expected Robert to agree angrily and speak of rallying men to defend them, but he stayed silent, staring moodily into the fire.

With a still growing sense of foreboding, Marian ordered the digging of deep keeping-pits to hide away their stocks of grain, oats, nuts and beans. Though Christmas came they did not organise the usual festivities, and the feast day itself was marred by the news that King John had arrived to spend Christmas with the Sheriff of Nottingham. Magda grew rounder and more restless every day and still Tom did not return from Derbyshire with her father. They heard that every pallet in Nottingham, every scrap of floor space in the city was taken up with a vast army of foreign soldiers who'd arrived armed to the teeth.

Marian grew tense watching and waiting for Robert's anger to explode, but instead he grew silent and grim, sitting hunched by the fireside, whittling knife handles until late at night. It was not the first time that he'd been like this. Marian knew the signs and worried herself to a shadow. When Robert had been in such a mood as this before, it had often ended with him going off without telling anyone and not reappearing for months. She wished very much that John and Tom would return; even Brother James who was so patient and good humoured could not lift the gloom.

'I don't know what bothers me most,' she confided

to Philippa. 'This terrible silence or his wild reckless courage.'

'Oh, I'd say he's much better charging madly about than only half alive like this,' came Philippa's quick reply.

'Yes, you are right,' Marian agreed with certainty.

The first day of January dawned, with heavy rain. As the wintry sun rose, the rain ceased and a damp cold mist drifted up from the earth. It was then that the real trouble broke. The first sign of it came as Gerta staggered into the clearing, her kirtle ripped and torn, young Davy in her arms, his head streaming with blood. Magda saw them from the doorway of her new home and ran to help, Brigit following close behind. The old woman panted and gasped unable to get her breath.

'What is it?' Magda asked, trying to take the young boy into her own arms.

'Terrible . . . terrible things!' Gerta struggled to speak. 'The King . . . he rides north, with his new found wolfpack.'

'They've done this?' Magda cried.

'Aye. It's punishment! My hut's a smoking heap, my geese scattered in the wastes. Everyone who rebelled . . . everyone whose manor lord rebelled, anyone who gets in their way!'

'What? What are they doing to them?'

'Killing them!' the old woman sobbed. 'Killing, burning. Burning the crops! Setting fire to stores of grain! My big lads have fled to warn Langden, for that is where they're heading. And my lad . . . my little Davy . . .'

'He's gone white,' Brigit pointed out.

'Get him inside!' Magda spoke with urgency, frightened by his sudden pallor.

Between them they carried Davy into the cottage and gently put him down on the pallet by the fire. Marian at once snatched up her water pot and a compress of clean lamb's wool. She set about staunching the terrible wound, but the child's face stayed deathly white, and her actions slowed. She stopped. The blood had ceased to flow, and the child who'd been so desperately rescued from the gallows died quietly there by the hearth.

'He's gone,' she whispered.

'No,' Brigit cried out, 'Not Davy!' She stumbled backwards outside into the clearing.

Gerta didn't make a sound but went to crouch beside her grandson's body. She wrapped her arms about his small shoulders, rocking him gently back and forth as though he were a sleeping babe. Robert looked on, his own face very pale. 'Who has done this?' he asked through gritted teeth.

'It's King John's punishment,' Magda told him. 'Punishment for rebelling, for supporting the charter.'

Robert moved swiftly to his feet his cheeks still ashen.

'They are heading for Langden now,' Magda cried.

Robert snatched his bow from the nail and strode from the hut. 'James!' he shouted. 'Fetch every weapon you can lay hands on! Bring the horses! We ride for Langden . . . at once!'

Marian looked up at Magda, a grim smile on her face. 'Whatever comes to us now,' she whispered, 'at least it will not be cowardice or shame.'

*

Magda went to lift down her own bow from its nail by the hearthstone, but Marian glanced out into the clearing and stopped her. 'No, not this time,' she said, her face determined. 'There is other work for us to do. See Brigit is at it already.'

'What?' Magda demanded.

'Come and look,' she spoke solemnly.

Magda went to stand beside her. The sight she saw was terrible, beyond belief. Though they had seen great sickness and sorrow there before in their clearing, nothing had ever been quite as fearful as the stream of poor folk who now wandered towards them dazed and desperate. Mothers carried wounded children, young folk supported the old, strong men wept helplessly. Everywhere she looked, they stumbled through the mud and wet grass with burnt hair, burnt hands and faces, all of them bruised and bleeding and as they watched the numbers grew.

Robert strode about, listening to their stories stony-faced. Young Brigit, despite her grief for Davy, already moved amongst them, giving help and comfort. James brought the horses round from the lean-to, stacked with every weapon that they had. 'Who will come with us to defend Langden?' Robert cried.

There was a great surge towards him and everyone who was able snatched bows and sticks and knives. Men, women, young and old shouting agreement till their throats were sore.

Robert went to Marian and kissed her. 'Whatever comes!' he said.

'Aye,' she agreed. 'Whatever comes!'

Then they streamed out of the clearing behind Robert and James, ill-prepared and ragged but filled with bitterness, a great swarm of angry woodlanders.

Suddenly the clearing was quieter, but now the gentler whimpering of those who were badly hurt, could be heard. 'Right,' said Marian rolling up her sleeves. 'Get that pot boiling, Magda, and Brigit, can you fetch buckets from the spring? We shall have to work as we've never worked before.'

Over the next few days they struggled tirelessly to give aid. Philippa came from Langden and told them that King John's wolfpack had set the barns and haystacks alight, but then moved on north with Robert and his gang hard on their heels. Isabel and Will had valiantly organised their people to beat out the fires and save whatever grain and food they could. In that, the damp weather was on their side. The Sisters of the Magdalen had taken all they possessed in food and medicine and left their convent, following in the wake of the trail of destruction. Now they tramped from village to village giving what help they could.

Magda was for once excused her hated task of grave digging as Philippa insisted on staying and making that hard job her own. Gerta buried little Davy, then resolutely set about comforting others who had lost family and friends. At last, on the third day, the flood of suffering newcomers ceased and some of those who had survived started to return to what was left of their homes.

'Today is calmer,' Magda said, stretching and rubbing

her aching back. 'But this strange quiet that they've left behind bothers me.'

'Aye,' Marian agreed. 'We might have a few days respite but then I fear the worst will come. They may live for a few days on rotting turnips but that will not last them long.'

Magda sank down on the doorsill, hugging her stomach. 'You knew,' she said. 'All that gathering and pit-digging, all that gleaning and fuss. I thought you'd gone mad, but you were right. You knew.'

Marian sighed. 'I could not see clear, as my mother used to say, but yes, now I understand why. I doubt we can feed them all, but we have good stocks hidden away and at least we may save some of them.'

Magda spoke bitterly, her eyes full of angry tears. 'They mete out the fast death first, then the slow death follows. Those who are left must starve.'

Brigit and Gerta who'd worked so tirelessly together came wandering over to the cottage leading a young girl who clutched a small rough-woven bag in her hands.

'Mother says have you a bit of grain to spare, or oats or turnips, or anything? For all our food is burnt and gone and father is hurt and cannot hunt.'

Magda smiled at Marian and struggled to her feet. 'Aye. Come on in. We shall find you something to eat.'

13
Creswell Caves

Even though Marian knew that they would come she could not have imagined how many there would be. The clearing was soon strewn with homemade shelters and smoking fires, for the weather turned against them once again bringing sleet and snow. Now they must struggle, not just to feed the wretched people who came to them, but somehow to clothe and keep them warm. Each day Philippa spent hours shifting snow and mud and digging up bucketfuls of grain from Marian's secret keeping-pits. Other women set up pots over cooking fires and produced huge quantities of wholesome bubbling stew, made tasty with nettles and garlic leaves, and carefully cut slivers of smoked venison and boar.

News came from Langden that the wolfpack had done their worst in Barnsdale, but not lingered to enjoy their spoils. Now they headed further north.

'They did not stay here for long,' Isabel told them, 'for wherever they set about destruction, they found themselves hounded by a strange Hooded Man and his gang of fierce wild wolves.'

Magda and Marian smiled. 'I'm proud of them,' said Magda.

'Yes,' Marian agreed. 'Though the members of this new wolfpack may be mystified, the woodlanders know that Hooded Man well enough.'

One cold January morning, Magda wandered around the clearing very early, for the wriggling of her babe inside her stomach would not let her sleep. Her ears picked up the clopping sound of a horse. She looked up with joy as the hooves beat out the familiar rhythm of Rambler's signal. She strode towards the entrance to the secret pathways, her happiness a little diminished as she greeted her new husband but no sign of her father.

'He's taken refuge in a cave near Creswell village,' Tom told her. 'It was hard to get him away from Derbyshire, for the people were setting about building up the defences of Peveril Castle, determined to withstand the King's revenge. They begged John's help and he could not be stopped from joining in and so I thought I'd best help too.'

Magda sighed, but smiled folding her arms. 'Aye,' she said. 'I can see it all.'

'Then the wolfpack came and went, and John is wounded,' Tom spoke with concern. 'Not fearfully I think, but he has an arrowhead in his thigh that I can't get out, and a sudden fever has come upon him. We travelled to Creswell, but I left him there, wrapped well and hidden

97

away in the big cave that Robert often makes his refuge. He could not go further and I thought perhaps Marian would come to him.'

'I shall come,' Magda told him.

'No, not you.' Tom looked anxious. 'You should stay close to home at this time.'

'Oh yes, I shall come,' she spoke determinedly. 'It is not far to go, and Rambler can carry me as smooth and steady as a boat. Marian has too much to do here, as you will see. John is my father and I will go to him.'

Magda would not have any arguments about it and when Tom entered the clearing and saw the desperate people who filled it with their shelters and their misery, he understood that Marian was indeed needed there. So with many instructions and warnings from the Forestwife, they set off just before noon, Magda perched sideways on Rambler's back, supported all about with rugs, food, medicine and ointment pots.

Tom insisted that he lead Rambler at a steady walking pace through the secret paths. The sheltering caves of Creswell, that had often saved the outlaws from freezing overnight, were not far to the west so that they reached the place by dusk.

The cave was one of many, set into the steep rugged valley sides known as Creswell Crags. A dark shadow slipped away from the cave mouth and into the surrounding bushes as they arrived.

'What was that!' Magda cried. 'Was it a wolf? Has it harmed my father?'

'Hush!' Tom said. 'Wolves have never attacked us yet,

though I did feel that someone was watching us when I was here before. This is a very strange and ancient place.'

'And still you left Father alone?'

'I had no choice, love, and though there may be others taking refuge in the caves, I felt sure that they would be more fearful than us. They certainly kept themselves well hidden.'

'I hope you're right.'

They found John shivering and talking to himself, half-awake and half-asleep, but he seemed to be unharmed. He did not recognise them, ignoring their presence and continuing to shake. 'I saw her,' he muttered. 'Grey . . . eyes like fire! Wouldn't go!'

Tom quickly got a fire going and brought water from the lake that filled the valley bottom, setting it to boil. Magda found it difficult to remember Marian's instructions and hard to stay calm.

'Where to start, where to start?' she muttered.

'Clean the wound first,' Tom reminded her.

'All right!' she snapped.

She bathed and poulticed her father's wounded leg, though it had swollen badly and turned dark purple. She fed him sips of the Forestwife's famous fever mixture, but the big man continued to shiver and shake.

'Wrap him up Tom suggested.

It was only when they had piled rugs on him to sweat the sickness away that at last Magda took breath herself and lay back to rest, leaning against Tom.

No sooner had she relaxed and got herself warm and

comfortable than her body stiffened with a sudden tight-
ness that pulled at her stomach. 'What was that,
sweetheart?' Tom asked.

Magda stared up at him, wide-eyed and alarmed.
'Perhaps, after all, I should not have come,' she whispered.
Then her stomach cramped again, so that she could do
nothing but gasp at the power of it.

'Is it the child?' Tom asked.

'Aye,' she growled. 'Think so! Must be!'

Tom hesitated for a moment, but then he carefully
moved aside and propped her up against a rug, protecting
her back from the wall of the cave. Calmly he rolled up
his sleeves and set the pot to boil once again, feeding
small sticks into the glowing embers of their fire. Magda
opened her mouth to ask him what he thought he was
doing, but another cramp made her shut it tight and grunt
instead.

Tom threw his small meat knife into the pot, then
pulled loose one of the bindings that tied the breeks about
his legs. He threw that into the pot along with the knife.

Magda gasped again as her belly cramped. Then as it
subsided once more, she groaned. 'Not here! I'm not
having my birthing here without Marian! You must take
me back! You must go and fetch her'

'I'm not leaving you and here will be fine,' Tom told
her.

'But father . . . he needs looking after?'

'We have done all we can for him for the moment.
What he needs now is rest.'

'Yes, but you cannot . . .'

'Oh yes I can,' Tom told her, smiling. 'It would not be the first time that I have acted as midwife. When you were a little babe and I lived with Marian, I helped with many a birthing. 'Twas long ago, but I do not forget. I know exactly what to do.'

Another birth pang came and prevented her from arguing more. Tom piled heaps of straw at her back, then he settled himself behind her, soothing and supporting her so that she could almost crouch upright. ''Twill not be long I'd guess,' he whispered. 'The cramps are coming fast. You are lucky!'

'I should blasted well hope it won't be long!' Magda snarled at him. 'And I don't call it lucky! You can damned well think you're lucky, to be sitting there behind and not growling here in front! You are lucky that I can't get up and thump you one!'

'Hush!' he told her firmly. 'Save your breath for getting the child out!'

'I'll save my breath for spitting in your face!' she cried. Then the sharpness of the pain took her by surprise, and an urgent downward movement, made her want to start to push the child out. 'Coming . . . it's coming! Can't stop it!'

'I knew it would not take long,' he said.

Magda bellowed noisily, but the child slipped smoothly out into the world. Tom was so busy, tying the cord and cutting it, then cleaning and wrapping the child to keep it warm that he did not know that he was watched. The wild sounds of Magda's growls and groans had brought them small and nervous visitors, curiosity overcoming fear. At last Tom handed the struggling bundle to Magda.

'A beautiful strong girl,' he told her.

They both looked up startled as light pattering laughter and clapping came from the cave mouth. Magda clutched her baby to her fearfully for a moment. 'Who's there?' she cried.

There was silence for a moment, but then they saw a small face with eyes that glistened in the light of their fire. Another face came into view, and another. Six small ragged children crept towards the warmth and glow.

Tom and Magda looked at each other. 'Were you there all the time?' Tom asked.

The children nodded. 'Aye, we were.'

'Did you see my baby born?' Magda demanded.

The children nodded again and though they were clearly still frightened they pushed each other forwards, holding out thin hands towards the fire's warmth. They were barefooted, their flesh blue with cold and terribly skinny.

'Where are your mothers?' Magda asked.

'King's men . . . got her,' was the tremulous reply.

'And your father?'

'Got him too!'

'Have you been living in the caves alone?' Tom asked.

The children shivered and nodded. 'Frightened of the big man!'

'He talks and shouts to nobody!'

'He's my father, you needn't be frightened of him. Give them bread,' Magda said as she rocked her child. Tom searched in the baggage that they'd brought from

Barnsdale and found some of Marian's fresh-baked, grainy bread. The children tore it apart, devouring it, whimpering with delight.

Magda leant back against the cave wall, exhausted, watching the children eating so hungrily. 'Well,' she sighed. 'If you saw my baby born, then that makes you her new brothers and sisters, don't you think?'

'Aye. Brothers and sisters,' they answered, smiling at last.

Tom sat down beside his wife and child, putting his arms about them both. 'You wanted children,' he said. 'Have you got enough now?'

Magda kissed him. 'I think I have,' she said smiling. Then suddenly a great bubble of mirth welled up in her chest and she clutched at her sore stomach as they both leant back against the cold cave wall and laughed.

14
The Gift of Making People Happy

When the first rays of sharp winter sunlight crept into the cave, John opened his eyes. He was warm and calm, the feverish shaking gone. He looked about him and thought he must be dreaming for there was Tom slumped in the curving back corner of the cave, his arms wrapped about Magda. They both slept deeply, but beside Magda lay a small bundle of soft woven lamb's-wool, that moved and wriggled.

John raised himself onto his elbow, gritting his teeth for his leg was still stiff and swollen. He stared about him at the six children, now warmly wrapped in Marian's rugs, sleeping soundly in a gently snoring heap, beside the dying embers of the fire. He turned smiling back to Magda, then laughed out loud; from the small bundle came a tiny tightly clenched fist that seemed to salute him cheerily. A small hungry cry followed.

Magda opened her eyes and stirred. She pulled herself up, a little awkwardly. 'Well father,' she said. 'You look a lot better now.'

'And it seems that your family has grown, daughter. It has grown quite a lot.'

Magda bent to pick up the small wailing bundle with the flailing fists as Tom stirred. 'You'd best meet your new granddaughter,' she said. 'We're calling her Eleanor after Marian's mother.'

John laughed again, delighted. 'Listen to her howl! Look at the strength of her little punching fists. Something tells me we have a future Forestwife here.'

The happy parents smiled down at Eleanor.

John turned, looking out towards the round shape of the cave mouth, lightening now as the sun rose. 'I must have been dreaming,' he said, 'but I thought I saw an aged she-wolf, here in the cave with me.'

Magda gasped. 'I knew we saw a wolf,' she said. 'I saw it slip away as we came.'

'Don't look so fearful, daughter,' said John. 'Perhaps I did see it. The creature looked straight at me with eyes golden and bright as fire but then turned her back on me, settling down by the cave mouth. I must have been crazy with the sickness but I swear it seemed for all the world as though she were guarding me.'

Magda fell silent and wondering, remembering Marian's story of her mother's wolf spirit in the woods. She hugged the new little Eleanor tightly in her arms, rocking her gently back and forth. 'Thank you Old One,' she whispered.

Back in the Forestwife's clearing the weather had turned so bitterly cold that each morning brought new deaths, not from wounds or starvation but simply from cold. It troubled Marian greatly that these people should be losing their lives for the need of warmth.

The day after Magda had gone Marian took Brigit and Gerta with her to raid the empty convent of the Magdalen. Brigit did not like the idea much. 'The sisters are our friends,' she protested.

Marian smiled as she strode through the icy paths. 'You do not know Mother Veronica as well as I,' she said. 'If they were here they'd give us their last scrap of food, their last warm rug. And I know where they keep their cloaks and the warm woollen habits that they weave and stitch so carefully.'

'Are we going to steal nuns' clothes?' Brigit was still worried.

Gerta put her arm about her. 'Believe me, honey. This is what the nuns would want, if they could see the ragged folk who shelter with the Forestwife. Their cloaks and habits will save many lives and without them there'll be more frozen corpses to bury in the morning.'

Marian knew the small convent building well and it was easy to remove the neat stack of woven nuns' clothing that had been prepared for next winter's use. Gerta had been right, for the following morning brought no deaths and for once Philippa did not have to get out her spade. The strange sight of old men and little children wrapped in nun's veils and habits made everyone smile.

Robert and James returned to Barnsdale in the middle of January with others who'd fought with them. They found the clearing quiet and organised.

'You have done well,' Robert stared about him at the orderly queues for food, the careful, industrious stacking of firewood. 'I dreaded to find it a smoking ruin like so many that we've seen.'

'Have they punished the people enough?' Marian asked. 'Have they given up their murderous task yet?'

Robert shook his head, his face grim. 'They head up north towards the borderlands, too fast and too many of them for us to follow. We have lost many friends. We are weary and bruised. Mother Veronica is returning to the convent; the sisters are badly in need of a rest. We wonder now what will happen when they return south, as they must eventually do.'

'Do the rebel barons fight back?' Marian asked.

Robert put his arm about her. 'Some do, some give in at the first sight of so many mercenaries, all well-armed. Pontefract's lord has surrendered to the king, and York and Richmond. They say Robert de Ros still holds out at Helmsley.'

'His serfs and peasants will suffer whichever way,' Marian said bitterly.

The men stayed in the clearing, licking their wounds, resting and feeding, though Marian's hard won stocks of food were beginning to dwindle. In the dark evenings they sat about the fires talking and fretting and making plans. Marian clung to Robert in the long nights, knowing this momentary peace could not last for long. A terrible quiet and sense of misery seemed to settle about the place, even though the deaths grew fewer. It was only the happy return of Magda and Tom towards the end of the month that broke through the gloom. Everyone was amazed and cheered that she should come back with not one child, but seven. John's leg still troubled him and Marian did her best, but even she could not remove the arrowhead.

Magda insisted that little Eleanor must have a naming feast and no sooner was she back than she sent the men off to make a swift raid on Sherwood. They returned with a cart piled high with deer carcasses.

'The wardens run in all directions,' Tom told them. 'Starvation makes the most law abiding reckless. The deer vanish from beneath their very noses.'

'Aye,' said Robert, smiling grimly. 'But we hear that the Sheriff has sent messengers to the King, begging him send a gang of his best trained men to put a stop to it.'

'And do you think the King will do it?' Magda asked.

Robert shrugged his shoulders. 'The Sheriff is no rebel baron, that's for sure. He's supported the King throughout. He'll find out soon if the King is loyal to him or not!'

'And we hope not!' chuckled John.

'Brig's Night can be my little Eleanor's name feast' Magda told them. 'And Peterkin is one year old, he must have his birthday celebration. Brig more than answered my prayers for a child, and we've had no Christmas, no mumming, no dancing. We must not let Brig's Night pass in silence.'

Marian hesitated. 'Well, we have plenty of venison to roast, but little ale to drink.'

Magda was in full spate and there was no stopping her.

The Gift of Making People Happy

'We don't need drink to make ourselves a feast. There's plenty of wood stacked and charcoal. We can celebrate with fire and dancing. Father can play his pipe and James can make a new drum from deer hide.'

Marian could not help but smile. 'What do you think, John? Is this giddy daughter of yours right? She's got it all worked out!'

Suddenly everyone was roused and laughing and fetching wood to build a big bonfire. They built it in the open space before the great oak: the trysting tree.

So Magda got her Brig's Night celebration, and they had a fine bonfire and ate and danced and sang until they were all warm and cheerful. Brigit sat quietly on the doorsill of the new hut watching them with little Peterkin wriggling in her lap.

Tom saw the sadness in her and remembered that Brig's Night had brought her mother's death as well as Peterkin's birth. 'Will you not dance with me?' he begged, sitting down beside her. 'Magda will look after Peterkin for a while.'

Brigit smiled sadly, but shook her head.

'Your mother would not want to see you sad on your brother's birthday. Now tell me? Would she want that?'

Brigit gave a great sigh and shook her head again.

'Magda!' Tom called. 'Come take the birthday boy while I dance with his sister.'

'I've been making something for him,' Magda cried, as she came over to them, little Eleanor tucked into one arm. 'We've nowt to give but love and kisses and . . .' she brought out from behind her back, a little wreath of mistletoe. She crowned his curly head with it. 'Come on, all of you,' she cried. 'All the brothers and sisters. We'll do a special birthday dance for Peterkin.'

Then the cave children followed her, snatching up each other's hands, while Magda took the birthday boy up into her other arm and jogged gently around the fire, her arms full of babies, singing:

> *'Mistletoe for happiness,*
> *Mistletoe for luck,*
> *Mistletoe for a fine little man,*
> *The sweetest little duck!'*

Peterkin laughed and chortled, his cheeks rosy in the fire-glow. His sister danced happily with Tom, keeping a watchful eye on her brother in case he tired.

Marian danced with James and then John, though she was saddened to see him limping awkwardly. It was only later when the fire was beginning to burn down that she went to Robert. The brief happiness that was all around was so bittersweet, once she'd wrapped her arms around Robert's neck she wanted desperately to keep him locked there, chained to her forever.

At last, as their feet slowed, and they began to wander exhausted to their beds, a strange distant honking started up in the woodland nearby. For a moment the revellers grew quiet and fearful but then Gerta roused herself from dozing by the Forestwife's doorsill, crying out, 'I know that sound! I know it well!'

She struggled to her feet crying 'Chuck! chuck! chuck!'

and clapping her hands. To everyone's delight her old grey
gander came waddling out from the bushes, still flapping
and honking, a neat procession of geese following meekly
behind. Everyone cheered and that made him flap and
honk more than ever.

Marian went to hug Magda as they returned to their huts.
'This was all your doing,' she said. 'It's done us more
good than the most precious medicine money could buy.
You'll make a fine Forestwife, Magda. You have a very
special gift; the gift of making people happy.'

'It's been a fine night indeed,' Robert agreed quietly.
'But tomorrow we return to shooting practice and sharp-
ening our knives.'

15

The King Rides South

In the third week of February the news they'd dreaded, arrived. Will Stoutley galloped through the woods from Langden with Isabel and Philippa following, driving a cart. It was crammed full of the very youngest and oldest Langden folk and two mothers with tiny babes in their arms.

'They're coming back again,' Will told them. 'The King rides south from Scarborough, but his men swarm all over the north in murderous gangs. Can you take care of those who cannot fight?'

'Yes,' Marian agreed. 'They'll have to camp out in the cold but at least they should be safe here.'

'I must hurry back,' Isabel insisted. 'We mean to be ready for them this time. Philippa's man has worked like a slave to produce arrow heads and knives.'

'Aye, and you'll not be alone,' Robert vowed. At once he was a bundle of energy, striding about the clearing, barking out orders and gathering weapons together.

The men left for Langden in twos and threes, as soon

as they were ready. At dusk Marian looked up from settling the newcomers and making them as comfortable as
she could. 'Where are the men?' she asked Magda, looking
about the clearing.

'Gone to Langden! Did you not know?'

'Has Robert gone?' she asked.

Magda nodded.

'He never said goodbye !' Marian whispered, suddenly
weepy.

'It is only to Langden that they've gone,' said Magda,
surprised at her distress.

'Aye,' Marian frowned, pulling herself together and
laughing. 'Only to Langden, and anyway when did he
ever say goodbye?'

The numbers of those who took refuge in the Forestwife's clearing grew over the next few days, and once again
the women had to treat burns and wounds and dig more
graves beyond the yew tree grove. Just as mercilessly as
before, the wolfpack harried the villages and hamlets of
Barnsdale, leaving death and ruin in their path. Sister
Rosamund and the younger nuns took to the road again,
giving what comfort they could, but this time Mother
Veronica stayed behind with two of the other oldest nuns
who were just too sick to leave their beds.

Marian's days were so frantically full of bandaging,
poulticing, cauterising wounds and mixing herbs that she
scarce knew what day it was and fell exhausted to sleep
for a few hours each night. She was up at dawn one
morning, wrapped in one of the nun's warm cloaks, taking
round drinks and checking who had survived the cold

night when she heard the familiar stamping rhythm of Rambler's hooves.

'I love to hear that sound!' she murmured, remembering how Tom had first come to her as a desperate, fearful child. And here he was now, husband to Magda and a brave and resourceful man that they all depended on.

Marian went out to meet him, smiling and hoping for better news but Tom's face was grim.

'What now?' she whispered.

'You must come with me!' Tom gasped.

'Why?' she cried.

'Get your bundles and herbs. Robert's wounded.'

'Where is he?'

'At the convent,' Tom was impatient with her questions and she saw that his eyes were wet with tears. 'John and I carried him there. We've had a great fight for Langden and chased the wolfpack off towards Nottingham. But Robert's got a sword slash, and we've taken him to the convent.'

'Why there?'

'We dare not stay at Langden. Though the wolfpack may be puzzled, the Sheriff will surely guess who the Hooded Man is who's defended Langden so fiercely.'

'But why did you not bring him here?'

Tom shook his head with sorrow. 'I doubt he'd have made it. There's no time to waste. Mother Veronica does her best, but says you must come at once and bring your herbs . . . she says bring all your herbs!'

Marian dropped the jug that she carried, her stomach lurched, then turned to the heaviness of lead as the picture

114

came into her mind of Agnes scrubbing washing at the blood red spring.

'All the herbs! All the herbs!' she muttered as she turned and ran back to the cottage, Tom following close behind. She snatched up her bundles and medicines, hesitating only for a moment before reaching up to the high shelf to take down the forbidden herbs. Tom spoke quickly to Magda, blowing her and the babe a kiss, then, without further ado, he pulled Marian up behind him onto Rambler's wide saddle and turned to leave. As he urged his horse to a canter Marian twisted around seeing Magda's white worried face in the misty morning. She stood by the doorsill with Eleanor in her arms and Brigit clinging to her side; little Peterkin pulling himself up onto wobbly legs.

'I should have given her the girdle,' she muttered pulling the stolen nun's cloak that she still wore tightly about her.

John was looking out anxiously for them as they galloped up to the quiet woodland convent. Marian leapt down from the horse and ran to him.

'How is he?'

John shook his head and looked away. Another wave of sickness swam through Marian's belly at the misery she saw in his eyes. But John himself was bleeding once again for the old wound in his thigh had opened up. Through force of habit she put her fingers gently down to touch the place.

John pushed her gently away. 'Nay! Go to him!' he insisted. 'Tom and I stand guard!'

Robert had been put to rest in the Prioress's own bed. The old nun was kneeling beside him, stoop-backed, her lips moving in silent prayer.

'Robert!' Marian marched in full of a sudden, senseless, bitter anger. 'You went off to Langden, and you never said goodbye.'

The wounded man stirred slightly and Mother Veronica pulled herself upright, reaching to kiss Marian's cheek. 'I'm sorry Marian, so sorry,' she whispered. 'I fear that now is truly your time to say goodbye.'

'No! I have brought my herbs and all my medicines!' Marian cried.

Mother Veronica bent down slowly and pulled back the blood soaked covering, revealing a deep and gaping wound in Robert's chest. 'Your herbs cannot mend that, honey,' she said gently. 'No Forestwife, however skilled, however devoted, could mend that dreadful hurt.'

'I must, I must mend him,' Marian cried, dropping down on her knees beside him.

Robert stirred again and groaned. His face was grey and his mouth tightened into a terrible grimace.

'Not this time, sweetheart,' he hissed. 'Not this time. Just hold me tight?'

Tears would not come, though Marian wished that they would. She could feel them there inside her, filling up a deep, tight well of burning anger in her chest. She took hold of Robert's hand and held it for a moment, then put her face down onto the pillow beside him so that she could stroke his scarred cheek.

'I can ease the pain,' she whispered.

Robert nodded. Marian got up and started sorting through her bundles. Mother Veronica brought a cup and poured water from a jug, so that Marian could mix a sleeping potion. As she started to feed it carefully to Robert there came thuds and the sounds of shouting outside. Then all at once came the thunder of a horse, galloping fast away.

'You stay here with him,' the old nun told Marian. She hobbled through the passage and Marian could hear her speaking fast and low with John. She returned grim faced and breathless.

'What?' Marian asked.

'The blasted Sheriff,' she told them, crossing herself as she swore. 'The Sheriff and a gang of King John's men. They've surrounded our convent and Tom has dashed away on Rambler to try to bring us help from Langden.'

'Do they attack?' Marian asked.

Mother Veronica laughed bitterly. 'They seem to be hesitating. I believe they're afraid to rush fully armed into a holy place. They're more afraid for their souls than of the Sheriff's wrath, but they will not leave us in peace not if they think they've got the Hooded One in their sights! John takes aim at them through the window and he's killed two men who moved towards the door. His stock of arrows is small but he has shown that he will not miss his target.'

16

The Last Arrow

It was clear that Robert could hear and understand for he groaned, making as though to get up but Marian pushed him down. 'Keep still!' she hissed, none too gently. Her mind was racing and her heart pounding like a hunted rabbit. Sharp cracks came as the Sheriff's men kicked down the low wooden close that kept the sisters' poultry safe.

'Sweetheart,' Robert muttered, groping for her hand. 'Give me your special herbs . . . the forbidden ones.'

Marian shook her head. 'No,' she cried, her voice hoarse and choked.

'Yes,' he insisted, struggling to make his words clear. 'It's time. The time has come. Don't let them take me! Death . . . it does not frighten me . . . not half as much, as to be made their prisoner.'

Marian looked despairingly up at the old nun. Mother Veronica turned away, her face full of pity, tears rolling steadily down her wrinkled cheeks. 'There is naught else that you can do for him, honey,' she shook her head.

With trembling hands Marian fumbled through her bundles, until the she found the one that she sought; deadly nightshade, all carefully tied in purple cloth. With trembling resolution she untied the bundle and tipped the dark powder into the cup, swirling it about.

'It might taste bitter, sweetheart,' she spoke through gritted teeth, supporting Robert's head and lifting the cup to his lips.

Though he shuddered at the taste, he drank deeply, then lay back. 'Hold me,' he whispered.

Mother Veronica turned away and left them alone, she went stumbling down the passage towards John. Marian climbed up onto the bed beside Robert, and wrapped her arms about him gently stroking his head.

'I hear the sweetest sound,' he murmured. 'I hear the rush and lap of the sea.'

Marian tried to smile, but a deep sigh came instead that turned into a sob. 'Do you remember Baytown, sweetheart?' she whispered, her eyes spilling over with tears at last. 'Do you remember how we lived together on the cliff tops there, high above the sea.'

'How could I forget it?' Robert answered, his face relaxed and smiling now. 'For it was there by the sea that the beautiful Green Lady first came to sleep with me.'

'We were happy in that strange, storm-battered place.' Marian made her mouth work, though her lips were stiff and unwilling. 'We should have stayed there and lived quietly together.'

'I would not have had it different, my love,' he whis-

119

pered. 'I am happy now. All pain has gone. It is only the bitterness of leaving you that makes me sad.'

Suddenly Marian was sitting up and reaching for the cup. 'It will not be goodbye,' she said. 'We shall not be parted.'

She gripped the wooden cup that was still half full of the deadly powdered berries and raised it to her lips, but Robert saw and understood. He lurched upright and smashed it out of her grasp. 'No!' he shouted, then slumped back onto the bed, as dark liquid splashed over her kirtle and down onto the floor.

Mother Veronica came hurrying back at the shout and quickly understanding what had happened, bent to take Marian into her arms. 'No!' she told her firmly. 'Not you too! He has gone and you cannot help him anymore. You've got to save yourself!'

But Marian pushed her away and struggled to her feet. She looked down at the motionless figure on the bed and saw that the old nun was right. Robert had gone, all breathing ceased, his face grey-blue and still contorted from the angry shout.

A thunderclap of furious rage exploded in Marian's head and she stared wildly around her at the sparsely furnished convent room with its crucifix and bare scrubbed floor. There at the bottom of the bed was Robert's bow and an almost empty quiver thrown carelessly down beside it, just one arrow left.

'No,' Mother Veronica cried. Seeing where she looked and fearing the madness in her eyes.

'Oh yes!' Marian snarled. 'Oh yes!' She swooped down upon the weapon and snatched up the arrow.

She strode down the passageway and before John could understand or do anything to stop her she was out in the bright sunlight of the woodland. She marched, arrow notched, bow drawn, out into the middle of the broken close.

The men were hidden amongst the trees, for fear of John's sharp aim, but they were shocked at the sight of the furious tear-stained woman wrapped in a nun's cloak, her clothes marked with blood and a weapon in her hands.

A horse moved forwards, its rider so amazed and stunned that he forgot to control his beast. 'Can it be true?' he murmured. 'The Hooded One a woman?'

Marian caught the glint of sunlight on his golden chain and laughed. She knew that gold chain, it bore the badge of office of the Sheriff of Nottingham. Though her hands still shook Marian took aim.

'One last arrow for the Sheriff,' she cried and let it fly.

'No!' John shouted.

'Yes!' Marian howled with delight, as the arrow sank deep into the Sheriff's chest. The man lurched forwards, the surprised look on his face turning to horror.

Then Marian dropped the bow and staggered backwards. She neither saw nor cared where the answering arrows came from but John leapt up with a bellow of despair as six arrows thudded into her body. She sank quietly down to the ground.

Though arrows rained all around him, John burst out

from the convent doorway like an angry bear his face white with rage and wet with tears. He did not hear the distant sound of galloping horses but whisked arrows out fast from his quiver and sent them flying like bolts of lightning. At each movement of a branch, at each glint of a weapon, at each gasp of fright, he sent an arrow whistling in that direction.

'Come on, come on,' he cried. 'Take me as well! You have taken my best and dearest friends. You can have me too!'

The sound of hooves grew louder and the air was filled with shouts. Still John moved steadily on towards the spot where Marian lay until at last he threw his weapon down and bent to gather her body up into his arms.

He expected arrows to thud into his own great frame but they did not come. At last he looked up and saw that the mercenaries had fled, leaving the Sheriff's body lying beneath the trampling feet of his frightened horse. Out from the bushes came Tom leading Rambler, followed by Isabel, Will, Philippa, James and Sister Rosamund. They stood there grim and silent as John wept.

Philippa moved forwards and sank down onto her knees beside her friend's body.

'Agnes was right,' she murmured. 'Agnes was always right!'

Bending over Marian, she reached out and carefully broke off the arrow shafts.

Mother Veronica came slowly from the convent, clinging for support to the frame of the door. 'Bring her inside,' she said quietly. 'Put her down beside Robert; that is where she wanted to be.'

They buried the Sheriff in an unmarked grave, in the convent's sacred ground. Though John complained, Mother Veronica insisted that it was done. 'I doubt that it will bring us trouble,' she said. 'Those with him will go running back to their pay master, the King, understanding naught of what has happened here. We nuns are Christians,' she said. 'And we are decent folk! We are not like them!'

17

Those who Light Up the Dark Woods

It was at dusk that a small procession set out from the convent. John, James, Tom and Philippa carefully carried the bodies of their friends, lying together in a new-made litter. Isabel walked ahead with Will, carrying flaming torches to light the way. Mother Veronica and the nuns followed behind. They set off walking slowly through the woods, heading for the Forestwife's clearing in the gathering gloom. As they passed the coal-diggers' huts close to the convent, some of the ragged, dusty children stood silently by a glowing wood fire, watching out for them. There came the sounds of their soft voices whispering, hushed and reverent.

'They come, mother, they come.'

'The Hooded One is here and the Forestwife.'

Then out from the crumbling hovels came the coal-diggers and their wives with babies strapped to their backs. Old men and women hobbled out on sticks and each of them, both young and old, carried a rush-light that they lit at their fire.

John was moved to tears once more and stopped, his huge frame trembling.

'It is too much,' he cried. 'Too much to bear.'

Philippa took his hand in hers. 'We are not alone,' she told him. 'You see, they tell us that we are not alone. It is not just us who have lost our dearest friends.'

John's wounded thigh bled slowly.

'You do not need to help us carry them,' Tom whispered. 'There are plenty of us to do the work.'

John shook his head and moved forwards again. 'Nay, I must do it,' he insisted. 'This night shall never come again.'

The procession moved on, and the coal-diggers quietly followed behind. As they passed beneath the trees shadows lengthened and the woodlands grew darker with every step they took. But though the night sky turned to black above them, a new, flickering source of light began to grow and spread all about.

Out from the charcoal burners' huts came more ragged workers. Mothers with children in their arms and on their backs; strong men with scarred, disfigured faces, missing fingers, maimed hands; hooded lepers stumbling behind, keeping their distance; each and everyone of them carrying a starlike rush-light. Their numbers grew and grew.

The word had gone ahead and by the time they reached the Forestwife's clearing, the darkest night was lit by thousands of rush-lights. The circling yew tree grove thronged with silent crowds that moved respectfully back as the procession arrived and went towards the burial ground.

Philippa and Tom set about digging the grave at once, for they feared angry retribution when the remainder of the wolfpack returned to the King. Such retribution could be terrible and desecration of an outlaw's body might serve as dire warning to those who thought they might rebel too.

Clouds cleared and a bright moon at last lit the clearing. There were many to help with the work. They made John sit with Magda, who refused to stay inside, insisting on sitting out there, beside the grave, her child wrapped in her arms. So father and daughter sat close together, tears coursing down their cheeks. They watched as they saw a deep pit grow that was wide enough for two.

'Agnes gave warning,' Magda sobbed. 'Agnes gave warning and I feared for myself, not them.'

'Nothing we could have done would have prevented it,' John told her.

Then suddenly Magda was anxious that all should be done well and properly. 'Primroses,' she cried. 'Fetch leaves to put beneath them,' she sobbed. 'And primroses to sprinkle on top.'

The distant sound of howling wolves could be heard as Gerta and Brigit organised a gang of young folk who rushed to obey Magda's wish. A great hunt took place in the moonlight and children emerged from the shadowy foliage with bundles of fresh picked primroses in their hands.

At last they prepared to gently lay Robert and Marian side by side to rest.

'Wait,' said John. 'There is something we must do.'

He bent with trembling hands to loosen the beautiful woven girdle from Marian's waist: the symbol of the Forestwife. He wept afresh for as he lifted it the girdle fell apart where the arrows had cut through the intricately woven bands.

Tears poured down his face. 'All is wrong!' he cried. 'This was meant for you daughter.'

Magda stared. She put out her hand, still cradling baby Eleanor, and took hold of the three separate strands. She looked puzzled for a moment, but then she smiled through her tears. 'No,' she said. 'I understand. I think I understand. This is right. Marian knew it should be like this. There is not to be one Forestwife, but three.'

The people all around them gasped when they heard her, but Magda went on, growing in conviction. She turned to Brigit, who stood at her side, calm and helpful as ever, Peterkin sleeping on her back. 'One is for you,' she said and quickly fastened the still beautiful loose strand about the girl's slim waist.

Brigit opened her mouth to protest but then closed it as Magda solemnly kissed her brow. Then Magda turned to Gerta who stood there on her other side.

'What?' the old woman protested. 'For me? You want to give it to me?'

'Yes,' said Magda. 'Your kindness and wisdom has helped us through so much and now we stand in greater need of it than ever. Will you stay here with us in the clearing, and comfort all those who are full of sorrow as you have been doing?'

A ripple of approval ran through the watching crowd as the old woman fastened the strand about her waist with shaking fingers.

'Now it's your turn,' Gerta said. 'Come help me, Brigit, and together we three shall try to be as good a Forestwife as she who we have lost this day.'

So they tied the third strand around Magda's still slightly thickened waist and little Eleanor's foot somehow got tied up in it too. There were smiles and whispers went flying through the crowd as they released her.

'That little one shall be Forestwife too, some day.'

Then more murmurs of approval came. 'Look at them. It must be right.'

'The Old One, the Mother and the Maid.'

'It is meant to be!'

Then John stooped once more and took from Robert's lifeless body, the worn and faded hood that he had always worn. He held it up, like a crown, so that everyone could see.

'We called him the Green Man,' he said. 'He was young and strong and fearless when he danced at our Mayday Feast. But then, when bitter trouble came to us, he led our fight and we called him the Hooded One. His spirit and his fight for justice must not be allowed to die.'

He swung round and held out the hood to Tom.

'But you . . . you should take his place, if any *can*,' Tom protested.

John shook his head. 'I am old and sick and weary of

it all. You are the one. This wound of mine troubles me sore. It is too late for me.'

'No!' Magda cried out. 'We will nurse you and make you strong again. Brigit shall mix up potions and I shall make you live for my child.'

'Dearest daughter,' he said, taking her into his arms. 'There is naught that you can do to heal this slow and aching wound. I am so happy to have seen this strong child of yours, but you must let me go now. I wish to return to the mist-filled valley of Hathersage, the place where I was born.'

Magda thought she could not bear so much sorrow all at once, but Gerta spoke softly to her. 'You must be strong and let him go. You must let a bird fly free,' she said. 'That is the only way that it can be happy.'

Magda sighed and gritted her teeth. She looked up from her father to Tom. 'Yes. You must take Robert's hood, my husband,' she told him. 'You must now be the Hooded One.'

'Yes, yes,' agreement came from all around.

Tom kissed Magda, then bowed his head and allowed John to fasten the hood around his neck.

The children came forwards and threw their flowers into the grave, covering the two who lay there together. Magda clung to John, while Tom and Philippa took up their spades and filled the primrose-scented space with earth, and piled it high.

Epilogue

As the first light fingers of dawn touched the dark woods, a lithe shape emerged from the undergrowth. A male wolf stretched and yawned, then shook himself so that small droplets of dew sprayed the grey stones and bracken all about him. He turned, giving a deep-throated cry. It was answered by a sharp, yipping sound, and out from the shadows of the undergrowth came a she-wolf.

The rays of the sun grew in strength, reaching in amongst the bushes and branches. The purple greys of night lifted, patterning dull clumps of grass with bright green and yellow streaks. Wood pigeons started their gentle cooing, greeting each other and greeting the morning. The she-wolf nuzzled at the roots, snuffing the earth and the damp air, her ears twitching as she picked up the faint gurgling sounds of water. She turned to her companion and licked his face, then gave him a playful nip, leaping high over his shoulders and past him, leading the way towards the plashing of a fast-running stream.

Epilogue

Water rushed over the rocks and poured down between two stones, making a waterfall that filled a sparkling, mossy-edged pool. The two wolves ran fast towards it, splashing into its swirling waters, drinking deeply.

As they drank, the light lifted further, turning the budding primroses that grew all around the pool to gleaming gold, and when they'd drunk their fill they climbed out of the water and shook themselves again sniffing the faintly flower-scented air. Then yapping joyfully, they raced ahead, leaping over dew-laden grass and foliage, following their own path through the awakening spring woods.

Author's Note

As with my previous books THE FORESTWIFE and CHILD OF THE MAY, this story contains a mixture of ideas from the earliest Robin Hood stories, life at the time of King John, and my own interest in women's history.

The charter that King John agreed and then revoked in 1215 later became known as Magna Carta. It was not until 1225, that King John's eighteen-year-old son, Henry the Third, granted the Forest Charter. This charter contained the much longed for words 'No man from henceforth shall loose neither Life nor Member for Killing our Deer.'

In the year 1216, where my story ends, King John struggled on for a few months, travelling around the country with his mercenaries, desperately trying to hang on to power. He lost many of his possessions, money and jewels in an accident in the Wash, then died at Newark in October of that year. As soon as he was dead, his household servants robbed him of his personal goods.

Disguise is one of the most powerful and repetitive

elements of the early Robin Hood legends. The story of an old woman changing clothes with Robin Hood in order to save him from capture is taken from this tradition. The rescue of the widow's sons from a hanging at the cross-roads is another old story which involves disguise, although in the original version it was of course Robin Hood that did the rescuing.

In many of the stories Robin Hood seems to have a rather unusual relationship with the Bishop of Hereford. Robin invites him to dine and teases him, makes him dance and takes money from him, but always lets him go on his way. While studying the period of King John's reign, I became interested in the many troubles of the de Braose family, whose members were persistently persecuted by King John. I was fascinated to find that Giles de Braose, brother to William, was indeed the Bishop of Hereford, and was also one of King John's most bitter opponents throughout the baron's rebellion. I could not resist bringing him into the story.

My version of the Sheriff of Nottingham is drawn from the legends and not based upon the real Sheriff of Nottingham, at the time of Magna Carta.

Close to where I live is the Derbyshire village of Hathersage. A large gravestone in the churchyard is marked as the grave of Little John, friend and lieutenant to Robin Hood. The local tradition is that Little John was born in Hathersage and returned there as an old man, after Robin Hood's death, at the hands of a nun, the Prioress of Kirklees Abbey.